where you belong

a novel by
Mary Ann
McGuigan

ATHENEUM BOOKS FOR YOUNG READERS

ACKNOWLEDGMENT
Many thanks to Rocco Mastronardo for helping me remember the Bronx.

Lyric excerpt from "LOVE, LOVE, LOVE" by Sunny David,
Teddy McRae, Sidney J. Wyche
(C) 1956 (Renewed) Unichappell Music Inc. (BMI)
All Rights Reserved   Used by permission
WARNER BROTHERS PUBLICATIONS U.S. INC.,
Miami, FL 33014

Atheneum Books for Young Readers
An imprint of Simon & Schuster Children's Publishing Division
1230 Avenue of the Americas
New York, New York 10020

Book design by Angela Carlino
The text of this book is set in Bembo.

First Edition
Printed in the United States of America
· 10 9 8 7 6 5 4 3 2

Library of Congress Cataloging-in-Publication Data
McGuigan, Mary Ann.
Where you belong / Mary Ann McGuigan.—1st ed.
p.   cm.
Summary: In 1963, when thirteen-year-old Fiona runs away from home and ends up reunited with
her former classmate Yolanda in an all-black neighborhood of the Bronx, their interracial friendship
gives rise to both comfort and controversy.
ISBN 0-689-81250-7
[1. Friendship—Fiction. 2. Race relations—Fiction. 3. Runaways—Fiction. 4. Afro-Americans—
Fiction. 5 . Bronx (New York, N.Y.)—Fiction.] I. Title.
PZ7.M47856Wh 1997
[Fic]—dc20
96-32026

*For Maryann and Steph, friends always,
and for brother Bill, a dreamer sometimes*

one

Mama had convinced herself—and us—that they would never go through with it. But the eviction notice said the marshal would arrive at 8:00 A.M., and he did. At first Mama tried stopping him with lies. "Mr. Levine said he'll wait for the rent. He told me himself. I spoke to him yesterday."

"I'm sorry, ma'am," the marshal told her, but he wasn't. He put his badge back into the vest of his dark suit and started his work for the day—October 11, 1963.

Mama's still at him, but Cait knows better. She's busy packing boxes, stuffing everything she can into the cartons Owen got from the grocery store.

This was our first apartment on our own, 1974 Mapes Avenue, just a little ways from Tremont Avenue, three rooms for the five of us. You can walk to the Bronx Zoo from here. It's the only place my mother could afford on her own. This neighborhood used to be all Irish and Jewish. Now there are a lot of Puerto Ricans, even some colored. Mama says they're ruining the neighborhoods, and the Jews are moving to Long Island. On Bryant Avenue, south of here, where my father lives, there are even more colored and Puerto Ricans. My parents get really upset about spics and niggers. That's what they call them. They act as if these people are taking something away from us. But really there's nothing much to take. Whatever it is my parents think we had, it's gone now. We hardly even look at each other anymore.

Cait's fifteen; Owen, nine. I'm thirteen, as tall as Cait and built like a pole. She calls me Carrot because of my hair. Liam's seventeen, broad-shouldered, as tall as Daddy, sullen. He misses the old neighborhood—Bathgate Avenue, up near 187th Street—where he could sing a cappella in the hall with Big Al and Guido. It was safe there, almost all Italian. Now he leaves his dirty clothes for Cait to pick up and sings Clovers songs in a falsetto voice as he struts through the apartment, getting ready to go out. By the time he leaves, he's his make-believe self. Tough.

But I know what's underneath. I've watched him lean over the turntable and place the needle on the song he wants to hear, slip his hands palms down beneath his thighs, and rock against the armchair's deadened springs, back and forth and back and forth to the rhythm he needs so badly. When he closes his eyes, all the feelings he's hidden come out in the way he sings.

Before we left Daddy, Mama sometimes had us sing

while we waited for him to come home. We never knew how drunk he'd be when he got in or what he'd do. Maybe he'd be sleepy; that's what everybody hoped. But mostly he'd have things to say, angry things that he'd saved up from days and days of not speaking at all or even looking at anyone. Then the slightest thing could trigger it—Liam answering back or Mama nagging, even a light-bulb deciding to blow. It didn't take much and then he'd go into a rage: lamps flying, tables crashing, and always, always Mama getting a beating. It was like a kind of roulette, except you couldn't decide not to play. You were stuck in the game whether you liked it or not.

To keep our mind off the fear, Mama would get us to sing together. There were nights when the songs worked even for Daddy, times when he would keep the door from slamming and stagger over to our circle. No inter-ruptions. No hello. Only the voice we'd forgotten was missing.

But now Cait is packing our stuff and Liam's cram-ming his 45s back into their dust jackets. He's already dressed, and has filled a gym bag with clothes. He picks up his skinny comb and slides it into his back pocket, tucks a can of Barbasol into the corner of the bag. He's got the last of our toothpaste, too. He stuffs his record case with as many 45s as it can hold and tucks it between the handles of the gym bag. Then he slips another batch of records under his arm, picks up the gym bag with his other hand, and moves toward the apartment door. I fig-ure he's leaving, but he stops at the closet first, the nar-row one by the door, and reaches inside on the highest shelf for something else he wants. I can't tell what it is because it's in a plain brown bag, except I can see that it's small, no bigger than his fist really. He sees me watching him and gives me his toughest look. "Don't you say nothin'," he says, then leaves.

I go into the bedroom and find the uniformed moving man standing before the dresser I share with Cait, gathering in his broad black hands all the little perfume bottles and jewelry cases we've collected. The clothes I forgot to put away last night are still in the corner of the room, so I pick them up. I don't want those hands on my petticoat, don't want him to see how frayed my panties are.

After he leaves, I go to the spot where the dresser was, my clothes rolled into a ball against my chest. The man has placed the things from our dresser into a shopping bag, and the jewelry cases have come open; our chains and beads lie tangled among the bottles of perfume. One of the bottles has broken and the smell of Midnight Passion in the room makes what's happening all at once even more ridiculous.

The flowers in the linoleum haven't grayed here. Balls of dust are woven around things we've lost, forgotten: an earring, a pen, a spool of thread. A fifty-cent piece is indented into the floor. I get it out and take it to Mama. She's in the kitchen, searching the bottom of her pocketbook for loose change. Four dollars, two quarters, some nickels and a dime lie here and there on the table before Cait. "Mama," I say.

"Not now, Fiona. For Christ's sake, not now."

The marshal's heavy steps pound through the apartment, echoing through the empty rooms. He hesitates in the kitchen doorway, uncertain whether to come in. Maybe he thinks there's something private about this family circle, some line he hasn't already crossed. "Is someone coming to pick up your things?"

"I'm calling a storage company," Mama answers.

"Better have someone stay downstairs until they get here," he says, and walks away.

"Fiona, you better go down," Mama says wearily.

The morning light is thin, hardly warm at all. The men have placed the boxes and the furniture on the sidewalk, and the two Puerto Rican kids from across the street are playing on the couch.

"Get off there, Carlos," I yell, and they dive off the back of the chair and scramble away. The furniture on the sidewalk makes me feel like a stranger. The mattresses and the cushions and the skinny-legged tables look alien. I don't want to belong to these things anymore. I can't wait for someone to take them away.

I sit at the top of the stoop, as far away from the stuff as I can get. Now and then someone passes by—someone about to have a day like any other—looks from the furniture to me, my legs held tightly together, my arms folded across my chest. I try not to see beyond my knees. I take the coin from the little purse I keep in my shoulder bag. The bag used to be Cait's, but now it's mine. Sometimes I get lucky and find loose change at the bottom. But there's nothing today, only the coin from under the dresser. I move it between my fingers, glad I haven't given it to Mama. I like the feel of it, the hardness, the idea that no one can take it away.

Liam comes over from across the street, rests his bag on the arm of a chair. I drop my coin into my bag. "Come on. We'll go home," he says.

"You mean to Daddy?"

"Yeah."

"I can't. Mama . . . what will Mama say?"

"I'm going back," he says, shaking the last cigarette out of a pack. "If you wanna come, I'll take you." He lights up, cupping the tip of the cigarette from the wind. He doesn't seem the least bit concerned that Mama might come out at any moment and find him smoking.

I'm afraid to go with him, yet the idea of getting out of here feels so good. "Will Daddy be home?" I ask.

"He's probably at the gas station. We won't see him till he gets in. Who knows when that will be."

"What if he's drunk?"

"He won't go for you." He takes a hard drag on the cigarette and waves the idea away as if it's no big deal. "I'm the one who'll get it."

It hurts when he says this, because we all know it, that Liam gets most of the beatings. He gets it almost as much as Mama used to, but that's because he steps in between them all the time, to stop him. Daddy never hits me, only Mama, Liam, and Owen, even Cait sometimes. I don't know why. Maybe he likes to have someone watching. When it's happening, I feel like I'm not really there, not even really in my own skin. I'm just a pair of eyes, watching.

"I can't leave," I tell him, and concentrate on my socks. They're Liam's, too big for me.

"Then don't." Liam gathers his stuff and leaves me there. He gets halfway down the block before I make up my mind to go with him.

We walk, saying nothing. I could be any kid walking with her big brother—a kid with a room, a dog, a phone number, things to do that day. But I know I'll never be a kid like that. No matter how many times we start over, the ache in our faces gives us away. I'm no one. There's no more to it than that. All I know is that it feels better with Liam, better than the smell of Midnight Passion. Better than Mama scrounging for dimes. Better than the sofa in the street.

two

Daddy still lives in our old apartment, the top floor of a two-family house on Bryant Avenue, a long way from here on the other side of Boston Road near 174th Street. We get to Southern Boulevard; the wind is strong here. I offer to carry Liam's record case, but he lets no one touch his records. He gives me his gym bag instead.

"And here," he says. "Have you got room for this in your pocketbook?" It's the little brown package.

"What is it?" I say, taking it from him. It's heavier than it looks.

"Belongs to a friend of mine. I have to return it." I tuck it inside my bag and pull the strap higher up my shoulder.

We pass Katz's deli. Even at this early hour of the morning, I can smell the knishes, or imagine I do. My fifty cents would buy us some Yankee Doodles, but I don't want to tell Liam I have it. I'm afraid he'll spend it on cigarettes. The wind is steady, cold, but he refuses to close his coat. I'm desperate for my hat, wonder if Cait has packed it away for storage by mistake.

We pass my school. It's too early for the kids to be there, but lights are on in some of the classrooms and I think I see someone in mine. I remember my homework is still in my book bag. No hat. No homework. I stop walking. "I have a math test tomorrow, Liam. Tomorrow's Friday."

"Not for us, it isn't." He pulls me along and I come more willingly this time, seeing that whether we go back or keep going is all the same.

The front door of our old house is locked and the bell is still broken so we walk down the narrow alley alongside. A porch off the living room of the apartment looks out over the yard, and wooden stairs lead up to a door in the floorboards. Liam can climb up and get us in because the latch was broken long ago, but when we get to the back, we see Daddy sitting on the porch. The sight of him scares me.

We watch, studying his movements. I haven't looked at his face in such a very long time, since long before we left him, and I'm hungry for it. Maybe Liam is too, because he doesn't call his name. Daddy looks old sitting there, afraid, the way I've seen him look around people he doesn't know, as if he thinks they'll see the kind of man he is.

He's wearing his gray work uniform, one leg crossed over the other, staring past the antennae on the rooftops across the way. He can't be up very long; his cigarette trembles between his fingers. I want to run then, before he spots us, go back to the stoop and the furniture, wait for Mama. Liam grabs hold of my arm and calls to him. Daddy shoots up when he hears Liam's voice and leans over the railing.

"Get up here, you two. Your mother's been calling Mrs. Olsen." He goes back inside to let us through the front door.

"I don't want to stay. I want to go back," I tell Liam. My heart is pounding and I can hardly catch my breath.

Liam drags me back up the alley. "Back where? To what?" He sounds angry.

"Mama's worried about me."

He looks at me like I'm a fool. "Then go ahead back. You can hide in a dresser drawer and let them put you in storage." We reach the top of the alley and Liam heads for the front door. I don't know where to go, what to do.

By then Daddy is at the door. "What do you two think you're doing?" he says, and I follow Liam into the house.

Mrs. Olsen opens her door at the end of the dark hallway, next to the staircase that leads up to our apartment. The morning light is unkind to her. Her face sags and her hair is brittle with the remnants of a perm. She wears one of those sweater clips to keep a dull green cardigan on her shoulders, and the sleeves hang loose. She looks at us for a second before she speaks, enough time for us to see what every outsider thinks of us. They're afraid of us, but they like it that way; we make them feel they're better than they are.

"Your mother called here twice. She's worried," Mrs. Olsen says, looking at me. She crisscrosses the loose sleeves over her chest to ward off our powers. "She said if you showed up here to tell you to call your aunt Maggie's house. That's where she'll be." She closes her door before I can answer. Aunt Maggie's house is up on Bathgate Avenue, near where we used to live, the place where I was born.

We follow Daddy upstairs. Liam takes the stairs two steps at a time, the way he always did. The banister feels good in my hand, familiar. This is the place we found to make one last go of it as a family, to give ourselves one more chance. The hope we had then seems so ridiculous to me now. I don't know what made us think anything could change.

The living room is nearly bare now. There's only one armchair; matching clown-face plaques still hang from the wall near the corner, the table below them gone. The lamp has tipped over on the floor, and the lampshade is dented. I remember the starched lace doily Mama kept underneath the lamp. I hang my pocketbook from the knob of the door that leads out to the porch, the place I always used to hang it.

We walk through the living room and into the kitchen. "Take off your shoes," Daddy says, "before that witch starts banging her broom up at us." We already have them off.

The kitchen smells like an ashtray. The table is a collection of playing cards, sports pages, crushed Camel packs, and dirty deep black ashtrays taken from the bar and grill. A pillowcase full of laundry is on a kitchen chair; an instant coffee jar is open on the counter, packets of sugar from the diner all around it, some whole, some torn. The floor is sticky with beer.

"What's gotten into you, running away from your mother like this?" Daddy is standing in the middle of the room, hands on his hips. The question is for me, not for Liam. This isn't the first time Liam's appeared on Daddy's doorstep.

"We got put out," Liam says, sharing the chair with the bag of laundry. I lean against the counter, hoping I can't really be seen.

"Your mother never put you out," Daddy says. He's at the table now, reaching for his Camels.

"The marshal. I'm talking about the marshal. Put us out of the apartment. The stuff's in the street." Liam says this as if it's not big news and studies the unfinished game of solitaire in front of him on the table.

"You mean evicted?"

"Yeah," Liam says, and moves a red seven onto a black eight.

"Jesus." Daddy sighs and sits down across from Liam, then gets up again, knowing there's something he should do. He shuffles over to me, touches the top of my head. I think he's about to comfort me, hold me even, but he doesn't. That would be ridiculous and we both seem to know it. He never does that kind of thing.

"Did you eat?" he says.

"We're all right," Liam says.

"You hungry, Fiona?" he asks me, ignoring Liam's answer.

"I think so. I mean yes," I say.

"Go sit yourself down, and let me see what I've got."
He reaches into the cabinets above me. His sleeve is torn
a little underneath at the armhole where he can't see.
"There must be something here."

I go over and lean against the table. Daddy pushes his
way through the cabinets, as if he's never tried them
before. He wants so badly to find something for us, as if
we're finicky guests who'll turn up their noses if the food
isn't just right. He pushes aside a bag of flour, a can of
lima beans, cursing them. He finds Rice Krispies and
comes back to the table pleased with himself.

"Get us some bowls, Liam," he says.

"I don't want any," Liam tells him. He's searching the
ashtrays for butts worth saving.

"Bowls," Daddy tells him. The tone warns Liam not
to disobey.

Liam goes to get them, and Daddy clears a place with
a sweep of his forearm. I'm altogether taken by his doing
this for me. He has me sit, moves a bowl in front of me,
then takes the cereal box and tilts it to pour. But he can't
hold still, and the Rice Krispies spray about the bowl, the
table. "Ahh, bejesus," he says, wounded. "I don't need to
be doing this for a big girl like you."

He goes to the refrigerator for milk, puts the pint
down on the table near me, then sits across from me and
goes back to his cigarette. I pour the milk and watch tiny
curdles nest among the rice. I look at him, and before he
can disguise it I see in Daddy's face what it must feel like
to fail, to know that you can't change anything.

I want to tell him it's all right, it's not his fault, that I
like my cereal dry, but I can't do it. I don't know how to

make words come out that way for my father. We never talk about how we feel; we only answer each other's questions, the kind about finding your sneakers or getting permission to go somewhere.

Daddy gets up from the table, takes his jacket from the back of a chair. "I'll go out and get you something," he says. "And I'll call Aunt Maggie, tell your mother you're all right. I'll take you over there after you have something to eat."

"We wanna stay here," Liam says.

"Here? Ya can't stay here."

"I ain't going back," Liam tells him.

"I'll tell you what," Daddy says. "We'll eat and go over to the arcade at Coney Island. It's open all year. We'll make a day of it."

Daddy is good at this, making promises that take your mind off all the bad stuff, the way you shake a rattle at a baby to get him to stop crying. He's done this over and over and still I'm always fooled at first. I think it's because it doesn't feel like a rattle; it feels as if he really means it. And I think he does. Maybe he believes he can actually find a way to keep his promises. When Mama finally left him, I knew it wasn't only because of the way he hit her; it was because she didn't believe him anymore.

"I won't be long," he says. He gets his wallet and goes out. I go into the front room, squat down by the window, rest my head on my hands on the sill. He comes out the front door below me, takes a few steps to the curb and stops, reaches inside his coat for his cigarettes. He lights the match and cups his hands over the cigarette to shield it from the wind. He tosses the match, and Mrs. Riley's dog comes up to him, his tail wagging wildly. Daddy bends and scruffs the dog behind his ear, says something. I hear Mrs. Riley call the dog away, and Daddy steps off the curb. I watch him cross the street, and I know the direction he's headed. It leads to Gerrity's Tavern, not to the grocery store.

"Do you think he'll be back?" I say to Liam. He's brought the box of Rice Krispies in, puts them near me on the sill.

"Not with anything we can eat," Liam says, and begins to search through his 45s.

I know he's probably right. "What are we going to do?"

"Don't worry about it. Once I see my friend tonight, we can get all the food we want."

three

It's hours since we tried the refrigerator. We've already eaten all the dill pickles, and there are no more crackers or peanuts. Cans of beer are all that's left, and the sight of bare shelves makes us even hungrier. Liam takes a can out, starts looking for the opener. I find it for him in the sink with the dishes, a foot of slimy, wet string tied to one end of it. The doily is in the sink, too, a dishrag now. Liam opens the can and takes it back to the living room.

I take one too and follow him out. He's picking out some 45s from his box, moving into his ritual. He's gotten the spindle onto the turntable, has the turntable spinning. He holds four records in his left hand, evenly spaced along his fingers. He looks for one more. It will have to be just the right one, and then he'll play them in order. The order has a meaning to him; it's like the rituals old Sister Mary Claire talks about when we go to St. Thomas

Aquinas Church for catechism class after school, the ones that drive the demons out of a person possessed by an evil spirit. Once I hear the first song, I'll know what comes next. The record drops; the arm moves. There's the expectant swish of the needle on the silent band . . . the Everly Brothers.

I sing with him. Liam likes it, I can tell, though there's no expression on his face. He just sings the song and drinks his beer, not looking at me. He turns the music up louder, sways with it, drinks as the second record drops into place. The Belmonts. He makes his voice go high like a girl's, the way Dion does. Then come the Five Satins. The Flamingos. Liam looks at the armchair, and I leave him alone, go to my old room, letting him pretend I don't know what he needs to do.

My room is only wide enough to fit a bed head to foot from wall to wall. The full-sized bed is pushed flush against the room's only window, and I climb across to look out. We left Daddy in the night after one more of so many rages, about six months ago. We took only enough for a day. I've come back since then to get my clothes, and some of my dolls. I was ashamed to want them so badly, especially my favorite, Catharine. So I forced myself not to take them all. I pick up Betty from the bed, the tall, blond bridal doll with the too-perfect face. Cait and I always made her the mean one. She's catty, hurtful. I can see she hasn't changed.

I reach deep between the mattress and the box spring to see if my old issue of *Screen Gems* is still there, the one with Elizabeth Taylor on the cover. It is, still folded back to the story about her and the singer Eddie Fisher and his wife, Debbie Reynolds. A few years ago, it was all the Hollywood gossip that they were splitting up over Elizabeth Taylor. There's a picture of Elizabeth in a bathing suit. I get depressed every time I look at this picture. There's nobody in my family built like her, and the chances of me ever looking anything like that are not good. I study the picture of Eddie Fisher, look at his ordinary face, try to figure out why she would want to bother with him.

I read some more, then look out the window. I see Mrs. Kushman come out into her yard to put milk out for the cats that visit her. She looks in every direction before she slips back inside, just like she always does, as if she's afraid she's being followed. I turn back to the magazine and read all the stories, even the ads in the back for increasing your bust size and losing weight.

I hold Catharine close to me and fall asleep to the rhythm of the armchair pounding against the wall and wake to the sound of Daddy slamming the apartment door. At first I think that sleeping in this place has made me dream of him, but the phonograph needle screeches across the music and Daddy's curses fill the place, fill the whole night—vile, mad curses from an anger bigger and deeper and more terrifying than any monster I've ever dreamed. I jump out of bed, weak with fear, desperate to figure out what I've done wrong.

I've known for a long time that it makes no sense to do this. Daddy being mad has nothing to do with me or with Liam or with anything we've done. But I can't stop myself from hoping that if I can figure out what makes him so angry, maybe I can keep it from happening again. I tell my mother, I tell Liam and Cait, I tell them all the time just to do what he says. Don't argue with him. Don't make him angry. I never make Daddy angry. I stay on his good side. I just do what he says. Liam and I should have gone back to Mama. We shouldn't have stayed. That's what made him mad. Oh, God. We shouldn't have stayed here.

I go to the living room doorway to see what's happening, but I already know what I will find. I've seen him like this before, over and over, louder and louder for as far back as I can remember. Daddy is cracking Liam's 45s, folding them in his huge hand. Some bend and pop into his face. Liam grabs for the ones that remain, and Daddy takes him by the back of his shirt, slaps him, throws him down. I watch. I want to scream, but I can't. When my father gets like this, the fear is like ice, freezing me inside. It takes over everything.

Daddy sees me in the doorway and stops. He looks confused, as if he's trying to place who I am, why I'm here. He doesn't seem to know me. His face is a stranger's face, the mouth all twisted, the eyes darting here and there, sweeping the room, searching out who will be next. It feels like a very long time before he begins to move toward me, a very long time that I stand there looking at him, searching for some sign that he knows it's me, Fiona, the one he never hits. He takes little steps, shuffling steps. *Don't hurt me,* I want to say. *Don't hurt me.* But I can't get anything out. I can't make him understand who I am.

Liam gets up, to keep him from me, I think, but Daddy pushes him down again. Liam must be thinking Daddy's going to hurt me this time. He must be thinking that. His mouth has blood on it, and he's crying, though there are no sounds of crying, only the tears on his face. Liam calls my name, but I run, leave him there. I run to the porch door and grab my bag. Out on the porch, I lift the door in the floorboards, climb down the narrow wooden stairs into the yard, then slip into the narrow alley. Leave him there.

A street lamp lights the opening where the alley meets the sidewalk, a weak light that does little for the rest of the alley. But at the top of the passage something catches in it, something leaning upright against stubborn weeds that grow from brick, a circle of black circles. I pick it up. The Clovers. I hold it with two fingers in that caring way Liam has, like a lover almost, and slip it between my sweater and my skin. I run from the house and let the coldness of the record center me, keep away the feeling that I'll break all apart. *There ain't nothin' in this world for a boy and a girl but love, love, love.*

At the top of the street, an old lady with a shopping cart is waiting to cross 174th Street. She's woven twine into the places in the cart where the metal netting is gone; some tape makes the handle. She rests against it, weary, and smiles at me, but it's too much of a smile, and I wonder if I've been singing.

four

I go south on Bryant Avenue. I know Bryant Avenue. It must be six thirty. It's almost dark. There are lots of cars and people. Some kids here and there. Some with mothers, most by themselves. I keep my head down, try to remember the sidewalk cracks. I pass the fire station on the corner of Freeman Street; two old men are talking to a fireman. The old guys are wearing heavy flannel shirts and hunters' caps. The fireman's in a T-shirt, as if to show everyone he's even less afraid of cold than he is of heat. I try not to think of how cold it is, how mean for early October. The wind is sharp.

I can smell Mrs. Nagle's fish store coming up on the corner of West Farms Road. She's out front, has on her husband's dull brown jacket over her long apron with stains the shape of continents. She's sweeping, sweeping, still sweeping the little fish guts and scales away from the front of her place, as if the slightest accumulation might scare away a customer. When someone approaches, she greets them, ready to lean her broom against the brick and escort them inside, tell them her specials. She doesn't seem to know who will enter and who will not. She's tense, her head moving quickly this way and that like a hungry bird's. I'm afraid she will remember me, but she doesn't. She looks through me as I walk past. I am not a buyer.

I go a few blocks more and cross Westchester Avenue where it meets 167th Street. I'm tired now, scared. This is way past where we were allowed to go when we lived on Bryant. There are a lot of Puerto Ricans, colored too. The stores and houses are pretty run-down. Something's in my shoe. It hurts, but I leave it there, not wanting to stop. The harmless pain keeps my mind off how hungry I am, how scared. My legs are weak, and I feel light-headed. From the hunger, I guess. I've been hungry before, but this is worse, maybe because it's mixed with knowing that it's up to me to find something.

I go a few more blocks to Aldus Street. It's badly lit here, creepy. Some boys whiz by me on bikes. They're making hooting sounds to each other, or to me. I'm not sure. They don't come back, and it gets quiet again. In the distance I can hear a radio playing, an announcer's static voice introducing something by Ike and Tina Turner. Across the street there's a bench facing into a park a block long. I cross over and sit down, look into the park. The place is dimly lit and shadowy, a set of slanted cold metal poles at the heart of it, the swings gone. The slide has a step missing. I know enough not to go in, so I just rest on the bench.

The songs are still in my head, Liam's songs. I let one in after another, let them chase away the scary silence. The silence is awful; Liam's face is in it, the bleeding, my name. In between the songs, I try to think about what I'm going to do. I can't stay out in the cold. I have to eat. I have to think, make a plan.

No one is around. I lower myself onto the bench, easy, on my side, so the record won't break. I find it then, settled between the wooden slats, hard and cold, a baby bottle left behind. I picture it getting tossed away by some ornery kid mad at her mother. I think of when Owen was small, the frantic searches for his bottle, always lost. Mama would hide it from him, hoping he'd give it up, but it never worked. He clung to it. Once he had it in his mouth, his face would change, go slack. Sometimes, if he was tired, his eyes would roll up, and he'd look as if he'd escaped somewhere.

The bottle is full and the weight of it feels oddly familiar in my hand. No one's here. It's dark. I can taste it once. No one will see. I take a small sip. The milk is cool and doesn't taste bad, but I put it down again because the feeling that comes over me is too scary, like a baby who's been left behind. I see now how alone I am, how lost, and I decide it's best not to look at where I am. Instead I stare into the night sky. But it is too big, this sky, too far away, and I still feel so afraid.

The wind changes and brings a woman's song, a voice like my mother's, and I know suddenly that I cannot keep from crying. I turn away from the sky and the bottle is there. I take it and close my eyes, settle into the bench, use my shoulder bag as a pillow. I try to focus on my mother's voice, but it breaks up and I drift into somewhere else, someplace safe, a place I can't remember knowing.

five

A great monster is gaining on me. I can't see him, but I hear him—a loud, shrill, awful moan, coming closer, closer to getting me. I open my eyes and can't understand at first why my back hurts so badly, why I'm seeing a garbage truck through the slats of a bench. Then it comes to me in a rush, and I sit up straight, afraid of who might have seen me sleeping here.

It's hardly day, but the window of the drugstore across the street is lit like a mirror. The sun's trying to make it above the apartment buildings on the opposite side. I get up and take a few steps, squinting into the glare. I look around, try to pick a direction. Something clanks and skitters against the sidewalk. The bottle. It's empty. I kick it away hard and sit down again. I don't know what to do.

I put a hand to my cheek and feel the deep crease there from the way I slept on my pocketbook. My eyes are still tight from sleep. Hunger hasn't set in yet, just a scary light-headedness. The garbage truck has moved down the block in the direction I came from last night. I watch it go and part of me knows that I must go back, if not to Daddy then to somewhere. I can't stay here. I don't belong here. But I see my father again, his hands reaching for me, his eyes not knowing me.

Something turns over in my stomach. The hunger is starting again. I should go to Aunt Maggie's. Owen and Cait are there now with Mama. I picture the four railroad rooms, lined one behind the other, every corner, every inch of space crammed with beds and bureaus and boxes and makeshift private spaces closed off by blankets on a cord. Aunt Maggie and Uncle Ed's kids hate us, all six of them. Even the baby cries when I come close. We stayed with them sometimes before we got the apartment on Mapes Avenue, times when Daddy would go over the edge. My mother would be frightened for all of us.

Aunt Maggie never says no when Mama asks to stay, but you can tell Uncle Ed doesn't like it. He stays away, works late. Aunt Maggie doesn't like it either. She yells at her kids all the time. The kids say she's only like that when we're there. She's scared my dad will come looking for us.

My mother is different too when we're at Aunt Maggie's, worse. She's on us like a hawk, always ready to keep us from saying or doing the wrong thing. And in a house where you don't belong, just being yourself is the wrong thing. To please my mother, I erase myself. I make no sudden movements, have no opinions. I hardly speak.

"Beggars can't be choosers," Mama said one night at dinner. I was sitting at a card table with Owen and one of Aunt Maggie's youngest. I didn't want broccoli and I'd made the mistake of saying so. Mama's words carried down the length of the three tables lined end to end, past the smug faces of my cousins, past the sad look in Aunt Maggie's eyes. A little beggar. That's what my aunt saw in me, someone with no choices. I hated the sadness in her eyes, but even worse I hated the anger in my mother's. It was as if to want to be a person, someone who liked some things and not others, someone who had a right to speak or even be, was inexcusable, a cardinal sin, a plot to make her life miserable.

The street is much brighter now. The sun has taken over, lighting the hidden places, drawing the people out of doors. A short, wiry man comes out of a doorway up the street. He's walking his German shepherd without a chain, and the dog trots along as if he owns the street-light, the mailbox. They come closer and the dog steps right up to me, sniffing me from behind the bench. "Schultz," the man calls sternly, and the dog stops inspecting me, but not without a warning look before he moves on.

I stand up, my legs a little weak, and go on up the street, in the same direction I was headed last night. I don't know where I'm going or what I expect to find. But whatever it is it's not at Aunt Maggie's. I'm not going back. Not today.

I follow Aldus about three blocks to where it ends on Southern Boulevard and make a left. The stores haven't opened yet. A man in a suit is waiting for a bus, a young woman shields her eyes, peering into a jewelry store window like she's lost something. I'm relieved there aren't many people around. I don't want to be seen. I keep my gaze focused just a few steps ahead, walking as if I've got somewhere to go, some purpose.

I turn down 163rd Street, thinking there will be less people, but there seem to be more of them, headed for the train to go to work maybe. I don't know. I take a right on a side street—Fox—without looking up. I study the sidewalk, counting how many steps it will take to be somewhere, to decide what to do.

"Fiona?" a voice says. "Fiona." I turn around and see her on the porch of an old house, her dark scrawny legs tucked around the posts, her loose red socks, the hi-top sneakers. It's Yolanda Baker from my old school, from seventh grade. I recognize her black eyes, remember her wild, frizzy hair, her dark, angry face.

Yolanda Baker was nice to me in school. I felt as if she liked me. I didn't have many friends. No one really knew me. I was in the school only five months. I was scared of her at first, like everyone else, including the boys. She was sure of herself, different from other kids. It was as if she wasn't a kid at all. She seemed to know something about grown-ups, about the secrets they keep, about the phony ways they act. She said she didn't pay much attention to what they said, only what they did. And the two, she would say, hardly ever matched. I knew that much already, knew it way before I met Yolanda. But I was afraid to name it, to say it was wrong. I thought grown-ups had a right to say one thing and do another. But Yolanda knew what it was, plain and simple. "Lies," she told me once. "They tell so many of 'em, they're covered with 'em, coated like a sticky second skin."

I didn't start in Yolanda's class until November. That's when we moved into the apartment above Mrs. Olsen. Kids told me stories about Yolanda, about how outspoken she was. I didn't really believe them. Yolanda doesn't look the part. She's kind of quiet, small, a lot shorter than me. Then one day in the school yard I saw for myself.

It was windy that day, a little raw, so for the last twenty minutes of the lunch period, when we were allowed to go out into the school yard, quite a few of the kids stayed inside. That made the yard a lot less crowded. Still, everybody went to the same spots they always did: the older boys in the back by the basketball hoops, the girls in the corner formed by the front gate and the half-wall that lined one side of the yard. The Puerto Rican kids had the south end of the school yard. The colored girls would be in the back corner, closer to the school building. The colored boys hung out just across the yard from them by the half-wall, back where the wall rose higher than their heads.

I closed my jacket when I got outside and walked over to the girls from my class who were already there. I saw Yolanda with the other colored girls, but I didn't talk to her. We really only talked in gym, or on the way home sometimes. She lived on Vyse Avenue then. That's a block away from Bryant. It seemed to be okay to talk there. But in the school yard, I pretended I didn't like Yolanda that much. Still, I couldn't help glancing over at her now and then. I wondered what the colored girls laughed so hard about.

I stood next to Terry and Betsy, listening to them go on about Mary and Elaine. There'd been trouble in school that morning between them. Elaine Goldman had cheated on the geography test the day before. She cheated off Mary Hennessy. I saw her doing it. They sat across the aisle from each other about two seats in front of me. I could see just about everything Elaine did; some of it was pretty weird.

Mrs. Kelsey must have figured it out when both Elaine and Mary spelled Arctic Circle with two *k*s. It was like the blind leading the blind with Mary and Elaine. Kelsey announced her suspicions for the whole class to hear and told them to think over what they'd done. They could see her privately if they wanted to discuss it. What that meant with Kelsey was whoever ratted first got to keep the passing grade. So Elaine told Kelsey later that she saw Mary cheating.

By the time the lunch bell rang, word was out that Mary had it in for Elaine. Mary wasn't really a fighter, mostly a whiner, but I'd seen her pushing people around now and then. Elaine was another story. She was the kind who'd pull your hair and knee you in the stomach. At least that's what everybody said.

Elaine came out of the school building first, and our corner of the yard got quiet. Just as she reached us, Mary came busting out of the doors and ran across the yard at Elaine.

The rest happened fast, like a blur. Mary pushed Elaine hard, and Elaine started swinging. After that they were just one big ball of legs and hair and skirt rolling on the ground, with the rest of us circling. The boys came over quick enough, but nobody tried to stop the fighting. Nobody except Yolanda. She tunneled through them like some kind of ferret and gave Mary the excuse she needed to pull away. That's when the whole thing took another turn. Reardon, the gym teacher, came out and decided—without even asking anyone—that Yolanda was responsible.

Yolanda told Reardon right away that she had it all wrong, but when nobody except Yolanda's friend Diana backed her up, Reardon said she didn't want to hear any excuses. I wanted to speak out, but I couldn't say anything. I'd already been called "nigger lover" for being on Yolanda's volleyball team. It wasn't a smart idea for me to be telling teachers who was fighting and who wasn't. Anyway I figured Yolanda could handle Reardon by herself. She didn't need me.

"Go inside to Mr. Rentko's office," Reardon told Yolanda, but Yolanda stood there, hands on her hips. "How come?" she said. Reardon told her they'd talk about that later, but Yolanda just said "How come?" again, like later wasn't even a consideration.

But Reardon wouldn't talk to her. "Just get inside, young lady," she said. "I don't have to give you a reason. I'm the one in charge here."

"That's all you got to say to me?" Yolanda said. She was fair that way. Everybody got a second chance. But

Reardon didn't take it. She said that'll be enough out of you, or something like that, and Yolanda finally went inside. Within two days, all three of Reardon's gym whistles were filled with glue, and Yolanda became my idol.

Yolanda calls to me again from her spot on the railing. "Hey, Fiona. You're Fiona." Her voice is up an octave. She wants an answer.

"Yolanda," I say. I barely get it out.

"No. I'm Yolanda. *You're* Fiona." Her skinny legs are swinging; the loose red socks around her ankles remind me of lanterns on ropes. She makes me smile, and it feels good.

"What are you doing around here?" She whispers this time, as if she knows already, as if we're conspirators and I have a secret that I've come all the way here to tell her.

I don't know what to say, so she tries another tack.

"How come you just left like that?"

I know she's talking about leaving the seventh grade last April and never saying anything to her about it, not even good-bye. She asks about it like it happened last week. I look down, remembering how I hated to have to go, to start again in a new school. Yolanda used to pick me for her volleyball teams in gym. She never picked the other white girls for her team, not even if they were super players. She liked to leave them on the other teams just to beat them. One time, she told me she liked how angry I got in the game. She said it as if she knew that picking me required an explanation, but I never asked her why. I was thrilled. She hardly ever lost, and I felt like a star.

"You still talk a body's ear off," she says, and jumps down from her spot. She lands close in front of me, looks me up and down. "You sick or something?" I shake my head no. "How come you're holding your stomach like that? You look like street rats nibbled on you for breakfast."

Again, I'm smiling, but how can I tell her about the record? People don't walk around with records tucked under their sweaters. She doesn't ask again, just steps back a little, keeps looking from my hand to my face. Instead of trying to explain, I take the record out, hold it up for her to see, casually, like it's no big deal, like I'm not a weirdo.

She takes it, maybe thinking I'm offering it to her. I reach to get it back, afraid she'll keep it, that she won't understand how much I need it. "Clovers," she says, examining the label. "My aunt likes them." She looks at me and hands the record back quickly. Maybe she knows I'm upset. She shrugs and moves away a little, toward the steps to the house. "You going to school today?" I don't say anything, and she takes that as an answer. "Me neither," she says, and sits down as if she's ready to make some decisions now, get the day under way.

"When did you move here?" I ask her.

"Summer."

"So you had to transfer too?"

"Yup. You hungry?" I think she wants to change the subject. The question makes my stomach growl.

"Yes," I answer, louder than I intended.

"There's eats inside." She motions with her head toward the rickety screen door. I look at it, afraid. I've never been in a colored person's house before. She waits for me to make some answer. I can't decide if I'm hungry enough to get over whatever's keeping me from treating this house like any other. It's old, the color of dried mustard. A maple tree, a big one, is very close to it. The higher branches reach over the roof; others block the front windows on the second floor.

There's an orneriness about this tree, as if it got here first and won't give in, not an inch. It hasn't lost many leaves yet. In the wind they tremble back and forth to red, then pink, showing off their backsides. I look up into the branches, caught by the movement, the sound of the dry leaves in the wind, holding on as if they might really keep from falling. I look at Yolanda. She's picking at a scab on her knee, paying me no attention, as if my being here were not unusual, as if this were where I belonged. This is the closest I've felt to safe in a long time, Yolanda saying my name, offering me food, a tree to look at.

Yolanda doesn't get up when I come to the steps, but she looks, watches me take the first one. The old wood feels soft under my shoe and I'm scared again. I think she knows it. "Cheerios?" she says, and I take another step. "Or maybe we ought to do up something fancy." She rises, passes by me quickly to open the screen door, and shoves her hip into the stubborn wooden one behind it. The door has a stained-glass diamond carved into it that I couldn't see before.

Behind the front door, there's an indoor porch. Boxes and toys and crates and odd pieces of furniture are piled solid and high on both sides, leaving only enough room for a tunnel-like path to the inside door. The second door opens into darkness. Yolanda breezes through, waves me on. I follow, letting the unfamiliar smells from inside close around me. They're not bad smells, but they confuse me. I can't connect them with anything. A gravy? Some kind of liniment?

The first room is big, dark, with lots of chairs. Not just a couch and armchairs. Ten other chairs must be in there, tiny wooden straight-back chairs, wooden folding chairs, a rocker. They're every which way.

Yolanda tosses one out of her way and leads me into a hall that goes to the kitchen at the back of the house. "You can get the milk," she says, as if she's chosen the easiest task for me. I open the refrigerator. It's filled with lots of things, neatly arranged. Not what I expected, certainly not like any refrigerator we've ever had. I take out the milk and look around the kitchen. It's plain, clean, uncluttered. A rush of shame comes over me like something hot on my skin. Even these colored people have a nicer home than I do.

Yolanda has the bowls and spoons ready and pours Cheerios and milk for both of us. I sit across from her and dive in, squeezing the soft Cheerios in my mouth, whole bunches of them, loving the familiar taste, the feeling of having my mouth full. Yolanda lets me finish two bowls' worth in silence. When I'm done she says, "We can play that if you want," but I don't know what she's talking about. "The record," she says. "I have a Victrola."

"I don't want to hear it," I say. It would make me sad, but I don't tell her that.

She doesn't ask me why. I don't know what I'd say if she did. "There are other things we can do," she says. "Come on."

I follow her out to the stairs in the hall, clutching my shoulder bag, and she takes them two at a time, sure of herself. I'm afraid and excited. New smells come at me again, almost like the ashes of something. At the top she waits, but only long enough to make sure I'm coming. Then she turns and walks the long landing to the next flight, a skinny, uncarpeted set of stairs that leads not to a landing but to a dark narrow door. I follow close this time, afraid to be left alone on these stairs, afraid Yolanda will disappear beyond that door.

I watch the muscles in her calves. They're strong, powerful. She's on her toes, trying to step quietly. When she's almost at the top, she stops, turns to me with her finger on her lips to hush me, as if I hadn't already stopped breathing. Dizzy, almost panicky, I reach the step behind her and she whispers, "She's not going to hurt you."

six

I don't see her at first, but I hear her humming, a big, deep, silver-edged sound that fills the little place like a hymn and makes it feel holy. I don't see her because she's leaning over a table covered with patches and patches of cloth and lace and trim in front of shelves stacked solid with more cloth and more lace and more trim all in so many colors and patterns that I can't make out where she leaves off and the patches begin. Then her great bottom shifts—she must have heard the door—and, still leaning over, she swings herself around to see who's behind her. She squints to see beyond the crooked half-glasses sitting at the edge of her wide brown nose and spots us. I hardly get a once-over, but Yolanda gets a dark, bad look.

"Mornin', Cas," Yolanda says, sounding as if she thinks she's welcome, but it doesn't look that way to me.

"You forgettin' what I told you?" the woman says.

She's upright now, the neck of a blond, blue-eyed doll gripped in one hand, a pair of scissors in the other.

"I didn't forget."

"Then how come you here?"

"Fiona's here," she says, as if this is something they were both expecting, something that happens all the time. I get another once-over.

"She for the readin'?"

"No. She's a friend of mine," Yolanda says, and the words make me feel solid. But the woman says, "Ahemm," in a way that sounds like she doesn't believe her one bit.

"This is Cas," Yolanda says to me. I nod to the woman.

"What kind of name is Fiona?" Cas says to me, but I don't understand the question. It sounds as if she's scolding me.

"Your people," Yolanda says. "She wants to know where your people are from." I still don't get it. As far as I know they've been in the Bronx forever.

I stand there dumb as the doll in her hand, so Cas says, "Irish. That's an Irish name, chil', isn't it?" real soft and gentle, as if I'm pitiful or something.

She turns away then, back to her table. She talks but not to us, quiet complaints about things in general: the needle she's lost, the pain in her back. She settles on the patches she wants and moves across the way to her sewing machine. The floorboards answer her heavy steps with complaints of their own—creaks and moans that make me think of amens at a Bible meeting.

"That for Mrs. Carson?" Yolanda is pointing to the blond doll Cas had in her hand, the one she's put down on the patch table. There are dolls everywhere. Some are outfitted in beautiful bonnets and dresses with crinolines and propped on stands or seated like royalty. Others, the ones without clothes, lie about any which way. I hate to see a doll left like that. It's not right. It loses all its dignity.

"She wants it tonight," Cas says.

"And you're hustling your big black bottom to please her."

Cas turns toward Yolanda with a sudden movement, and the chair falls. She looks at Yolanda, then at me. Yolanda jumps away, apologizing before the old lady can make another move. "I don't want no mo' apologizin' from you." Her voice sounds as if she's holding something in, something she wants to say but can't. Maybe because of me.

Yolanda rights the chair and stands before Cas with her hands clasped behind her like a soldier awaiting orders. "I'll take it over for you." She seems to want to make amends. Cas doesn't answer, just settles herself in front of the machine and makes it buzz softly.

I can't take my eyes off her hands. She works so fast, the dark, thick fingers feeding the material to the needle, taking it this way and that, as if they have their movements memorized. Now and then, beyond the needle, the pale palm waits to feel the rightness of the ruffle, to inspect the needle's work. When she's satisfied, she pulls the piece away—some kind of apron—and cuts the thread to free it clear.

"Fetch that doll, chil'," Cas says to me, and points. It's

the blue-eyed one she means, the one she left on the table. I hurry to get it, thrilled to be a part of what she's doing. She tucks the apron once around the blonde's waist, seems satisfied. She rises, humming again, and moves to a worktable where outfits are lying all about. Some are nearly finished, others just begun. She finds a royal blue dress and tries the lacy apron over it. It's beautiful. Just beautiful. She seems to know it, too, because she makes a sound like she's pleased.

She looks at me beside her and says, "What do you think?" She says it as if it really matters to her.

"It's . . . oh . . . I love it," is all I can say.

She smiles a big white smile. I can see a little silver tooth toward the corner of her mouth. "You have dolls?"

I feel as if I'm too big for my dolls, too old to be caught playing with them, and I almost tell her no. "Yes, we—me and my sister—we have a lot of dolls. A whole collection, kind of. Every year for Christmas and for our birthdays she gets a dark-haired one and I get a red-haired one."

She raises her eyebrows as if she's impressed. "Well, I can see why," she says, looking at my hair. "I'd like to see them sometime." I feel lonely hearing her say that; I wonder what I'm doing here, away from my dolls, away from everything. When I heard Daddy yelling and ran to the doorway, I stepped on something. Catharine. It must have been Catharine, her straw hat. It was the straw hat crushing under my sneaker. I feel weak suddenly from the thought of it, and my eyes are burning. I don't know how Cas can tell what's going on inside me, but she squeezes my hand, tells me to sit and rest, says how she likes company. I like her.

Yolanda comes and stands beside me, leaning carelessly against the outfits on the worktable. "When do you think you'll be done?" she says to Cas.

"Be done when I'm done."

"What time? If you want me to walk it over, I need to know a time." Yolanda's voice is a little shrill, and she's moving her leg in time to some rhythm inside of her, impatient for an answer.

"Didn't say I wanted you to."

Yolanda groans and moves away from us, seems to give up on Cas. "You coming?" she says, talking to me.

I nod and move toward her; she's got the door open. I want to stay here, but I can't say it. I don't belong here. I don't belong anywhere, but at least Yolanda seems to expect me to be with her, and that's something anyway. Yolanda is already several steps down when Cas says, "Be done round three or so."

"Yes, ma'am," Yolanda says.

Cas looks at me in the doorway. "Pleasure meetin' you, Fiona," she says.

"Thank you," I say.

"You come by again," she says. And I feel all at once lost, displaced, not sure if it's okay to want to do that.

Yolanda goes all the way downstairs into the front room, the room with all the wooden chairs, and sits down in one. I follow her in and sit across from her, but a few chairs away. Neither of us speaks for a while. We look like mourners at a wake.

"So?" she says, fixing the barrette that holds her hair back.

"So?" I answer back.

"You're really not going to school?" She's staring at me, examining me almost, with that no-nonsense look of hers.

"I can't," I say, and look away, but I can feel her dark eyes on me.

"How come?"

"It's too far away."

"So how come you're so far away from it?"

"I was at my father's."

"How come you're not there now?"

I know I should make something up, about how I got here and why I'm not going to school, but I can't think of any way to explain it all. "I decided I don't want to be with them right now." Saying it, I realize that there really is no other way to describe it. Yolanda looks impressed, looks at me the way she did when I would spike somebody's return over the volleyball net.

"So where you going to live?"

I shrug. She smiles at this, looks at me like I'm something wild.

"How come you have so many chairs in here?" I ask.

"They're my aunt's."

"Oh," I say, as if that explains everything.

"She teaches in here." Yolanda says this with pride.

"Teaches?"

"Reading. Lots of folks can't read. So she teaches 'em. Mostly kids. Some grown-ups."

I look around, try to imagine what it would be like to learn something in here instead of in dull green classrooms, with the same old dusty alphabet buckling away from the walls over our heads and everybody's social studies tests pinned to the bulletin boards as if they were something worth looking at. This room is quiet, shadowy, as if it's got secrets, things you might really want to know, things somebody cares about. The walls are papered with dark flowers, and the wooden mantel of the fireplace is taller than I am. The hearth is crowded with plants in clay pots, the carpet so thin you can see spots of the floor through it.

"Won't you get in trouble if you don't show up for school?" I ask her, shifting in my chair. It's hard and uncomfortable.

"With who?" she says.

"Your mother?"

"Got no mother." It's her turn to look away this time.

"What happened to her?" I ask, because I know she has one. I've seen her. She's always dressed up, like maybe she works in Manhattan.

"She's gone." She grips the seat of her chair and swings her legs high and fast. I aim my toes up, but I can't do the same without stubbing my heels into the thin carpet.

"Where?" I can't help asking.

"Doesn't make any difference where," she says, still swinging her legs.

"Your father, then?"

"There's no father. There's nobody," she says flatly.

"Who takes care of you?"

She gets still, looks at me sharply, pounds her thumb into her chest, as if to make sure I get it straight this time. "*I* take care of me."

"What about Cas?"

"She cooks for us."

"She's not your grandmother?"

"There's nobody. I told you."

"Your aunt?"

"I take care of me. My aunt doesn't pay me any mind." She gets quiet, so I stop the questions. "She's mostly on the road anyway."

"On the road where?"

"Wherever there's a march." Yolanda sticks her chin out at me, as if daring me with this news, but I don't know what she's talking about.

"A march?"

She can see I don't get it. "Don't you watch TV? Montgomery? Birmingham?"

"You mean a civil rights march?" I can hardly believe it. I can't make sense of it. My parents are always saying it's Communists who go on those marches. But Yolanda's just an ordinary person. Her aunt can't be a Communist.

"She got beaten up at the last one," Yolanda says.

"Beat up?" I look at Yolanda more closely, to see if there's something about her I may have missed before. But I don't even know what to look for. I don't even know what Communists look like.

"People get beat up a lot more than they show on TV," she says.

"Why?"

"You playin' with me, girl?" She sounds annoyed.

"No."

She looks down, and I don't understand what's wrong. Maybe I shouldn't ask her any more questions. Maybe she's touchy about being colored. She looks up again, and her face is different. Her eyebrows are scrunched together and her mouth is in a pout. She looks mad at me.

"White folks have been beating on niggers for a long time."

I stare at her, confused.

"That's what Cheryl says."

"Cheryl?"

"My aunt."

I don't know what to say. I've never beaten anyone up. Of any color. And I'm pretty sure my father doesn't beat up anyone else but us.

"She shows me newspaper stories about it," Yolanda says. "The stories don't tell it all, though, not what really happens."

"Has she ever gotten really hurt?"

"Some bleeding. That's all. Her friend got hurt bad last time, though."

"Yeah?"

"Died."

"God."

"God doesn't seem too bothered about it," she says, sounding a little angry. I think that myself sometimes, that God isn't exactly losing sleep over us, the way the nuns in catechism class after school make it sound.

"What did she do?" I say.

"Who?"

"Your aunt's friend? What was she doing that they beat her up like that?"

"It wasn't a she; it was a he. And he was eating his lunch at a counter in a store. Except it was a counter for white folks." Her voice does something with the word "white" that makes me uncomfortable. "Anyway what makes you think you have to be doing something wrong to get killed? You just have to be black enough, that's all." And there's that look in her eyes, the one that makes everyone so careful around Yolanda, so scared, the one I saw across the net in our first game, the one that made me want to be like her.

On TV the police in Birmingham opened up fire hoses on the colored people, set dogs on them. They were young like me, like Liam; the water blew them off their feet like they were paper dolls. But watching people get hurt on TV doesn't feel the same as watching it in real life. On TV, a part of me doesn't really believe it, even while I'm seeing it happen; when I see someone get hurt for real, I know it's happening because it takes over everything else. I can't see anything or hear anything else but the hurt. I don't stop believing it till later, after it's over.

The last time Daddy beat up Mama was just before we left him; she can't hear in her left ear so good now. That makes it harder for me to forget it happened. Every time she says, "What?" or "Speak up," I see his hand in the air again, the huge paw like a baseball mitt, sudden, yet you knew it was coming, then the snap of her head back, the look on her face as if she can't believe he's hit her. And that awful feeling takes over, the one I always have when she gets hit, like I can feel the blows. Or maybe it's that I want to feel them. Anything to keep her from getting hurt anymore. But I'm not the one. I'm not the one he goes after. I'm the witness, the one who does nothing, the one without the courage.

Yolanda gets up and goes to the window. "So how'd you wind up here?" she says, and parts the curtain a little to look out.

"I told you. I don't want to be with them anymore."

"How come?"

Yolanda's question is simple. I want to squirm away from it, but feel she won't let me.

"'Cause . . . 'cause I don't want to stay with my father, and we haven't got a place anymore."

"I don't get it," she says, looking not at me but at something outside in the street.

I get up, cross over to the fireplace to get a better look at the plants. I can still feel the hardness of the wooden chair on my back. I'm glad Yolanda's not looking at me. It makes it easier to say it. "My mom . . . she couldn't pay the rent."

"Huh?"

"When you . . . when you can't pay the rent, they make you leave your place." I sneak a side look at her, expecting she'll laugh, cry, who knows. What's a person supposed to do when you tell them something like this?

She lets the curtain go, turns away from the window. "I know what you're talking about." Her voice sounds

47

different, softer. "That happened to Willy. Willy Johnson. He's with his grandma now. South Carolina. He was in our class. You remember? He always wore those loafers to gym, bugged the shit out of Reardon."

My throat is closed up; I can't say any more. I can't even believe I've said what I've said, that now someone knows what's happened to us. It feels as if I've been shoved out onto a stage—or into an arena like the Romans had for their slaves, all exposed for the crowds to jeer at.

Yolanda comes over to me, real close, stands with her hands on her hips and her chin jutting out. Her eyes have no smile in them at all. "You're going to be with me today?" She says it like a dare, like this is something I have a choice about. But it isn't like that. I am where I am. I never planned to be here, and I have no plans to leave. So I say "yes," and she says "good," as if she knows just what we ought to do. And that's better than anything else I have right now.

seven

Yolanda takes me west on 163rd Street to Westchester Avenue, and we race down the street. Yolanda sometimes gets a little bit ahead of me and I trail along, trying to lower my head down into the jacket so my ears won't feel so cold. She got the coat for me from her aunt's closet. She offered me a hat too, but she didn't take one, so I didn't want one either. The sleeves of the jacket fall past my hands, so I can keep my fists tucked out of the wind. Yolanda says the jacket belongs to her aunt, but it seems like a boy's jacket, a team jacket, green and gold with " '61" on the shoulder.

We get to Prospect Avenue and make a left. Yolanda hasn't told me where we're going, and I don't really care, except that nearly everyone we pass now is colored, and I'm starting to feel like I don't belong. We come to a drearier part of the avenue. There are men in doorways and stores closed down all along the street, and I wish Yolanda would stay closer. I've never been this many blocks south of Bryant Avenue before. This is the neighborhood my family talks about, the one south of Crotona Park, the one they say the spics and niggers have taken over. "Where are we going, anyway?" I ask her.

"We're just walking."

She looks back at me every little while, and I can tell she's thinking about something, trying to make up her mind. She moves toward the entrance of what used to be a dry cleaners and motions me to sit down with her on the step. She gives me a serious look. "You any good at keeping your mouth shut?"

"You mean secrets?" I say. "I can keep a secret." And I laugh inside. She doesn't know she's talking to an expert. My whole life is a secret.

"Bigger than secrets. I'm not talking about piss-ass girlie stuff. This isn't about who likes whose blue eyes this week. I'm talking about something else altogether, the kind of stuff you can *never* tell."

So am I. But I don't bother saying it. I just nod. She believes me, I can tell. But still she says, " 'Cause if you do, you can get hurt," and her voice is scary. "You know what I'm talking about?"

I nod again, thinking about the secrets that hurt you either way, whether you tell them or not. Like when I couldn't tell Mama that Daddy beat up Owen again, because the whole thing would only start all over, with her getting it too.

I know what she's talking about. I know all about the

things you don't say out loud, but I'm glad she doesn't make me say so.

She gets up, and I do too. We walk another block or so. The sun feels brighter, stronger. There's a hint of that special October light in it, even here where everything looks so gray and shadowy. I've seen the real October light, on a zillion leaves on a million trees, turning them every color you can imagine. Not just gold or brown the way it is around here, but electric reds and oranges.

Daddy got a station wagon from some friend a few years ago, fifth grade, and he took us all up to Vermont by a lake. There we were, with hills on every side, mountains really. And late in the afternoon the light turned golden. I went off alone for a while, to have it for myself. All around me, the trees were lit with it, each leaf separate in the light.

"This is it," Yolanda says. We've come to a coffee shop. A tall, skinny boy, not much older than us, is leaning against the wall that forms the narrow recessed entrance. He's got a cigarette hanging from his mouth and a black hat with a narrow brim, a man's hat, and he's facing the street. He makes a comical partner for the blue-eyed girl in the Coca-Cola ad nailed to the wall. She's got a shiny blond pageboy, and she's happy with herself and her Coke. The boy doesn't look happy with anything.

Yolanda nods to him and heads for the door beside the coffee shop, the one that leads to the apartment upstairs. The boy looks at me but speaks to Yolanda. "Where you goin'?"

"We're going up," she says, and moves as if to pass him.

"*You* goin' up," he says, grabbing her arm. "She ain't."

"She's okay. She's my friend," Yolanda says, trying to sound casual.

The boy shakes his head no, sets his dark, determined eyes back on the street again. "Ain't mine."

"Come on, Leon." Yolanda's voice is whiny.

He shakes his head again, but doesn't look at her.

For some reason, Yolanda doesn't want to give the kid a hard time. She turns and tells me that I'll have to wait for her down here.

"No," I tell her, grasping my pocketbook closer to my side.

"I'll be right down. It only takes a second."

I want to ask her what she's talking about, what all the silly mystery is about, but Leon is standing there like part of the wall, absorbing everything, his dark eyes moving from us to the street, to the cars passing by. Yolanda's inside the door before I can say anything, and I'm left there with Leon and the Coca-Cola girl.

I move over to the curb and lean against a parked car. I'm desperate to know how many blocks I am from Daddy's place. Thirty maybe? From Aunt Maggie's house on Bathgate, even more. I look at Leon, and I feel a lot farther away than that. He sneaks a glance at me now and then, a cigarette dangling from his lip, arms folded across his chest. I think he hates me. Just then the car I'm leaning on starts up, a big rumbling blast that startles me so much I jump away, trip and fall. My knee hurts, and my face is hot with embarrassment. Leon's shiny shoes come alongside me. I don't look up, but he reaches his hand down to help me. I take it, fascinated for the moment by how dark his skin is next to mine.

When I'm up, he hands me my pocketbook. I say thank you, but he only flicks his cigarette butt into the street, as if he's disgusted with me, or maybe with everything. He doesn't look at me, just seems satisfied that I'm all right and says something I can't understand to the driver, who hasn't pulled away yet, then goes back to his post.

Last summer colored people were holding hands with whites, holding hands and singing, marching. Right in Washington, D.C., right on TV. Leon doesn't look like he wants to hold hands with anyone. Just a couple of weeks after the march, somebody bombed a church in Birmingham, killed some girls in Sunday school, girls my age. Maybe that's why he hates me.

The door opens and Yolanda is out again, breathless. She waves good-bye to Leon, grabs my coat sleeve. "Come on. We've got to hurry."

"Where?"

But Yolanda doesn't answer me. She gets one hand under my arm and keeps the other in the pocket of her jacket. We move fast, and turn down 150th Street. It's narrow, gray, like everything else except the sky. I see a barber pole halfway down the block, and that's where Yolanda stops, just a little away from the shop. She keeps her hands in her pockets and looks intently up the street. It's empty. Nothing. "What are we doing here?" I ask her.

"It won't take long."

A car turns down the top of the block. Yolanda leans forward to look at it, as if she's expecting a lift. The car moves past us, an old blue Chevy with the silver front bumpers that look like a bulldog's teeth. The front license plate is hanging by one screw. An old man's driving.

The car continues down the street, and it's quiet again. The barber pole hums, the red stripes winding their way to the bottom to disappear again and again. Across the street, the door at the top of a stoop opens and a shopping cart comes onto the landing, the frail woman behind the cart struggling to keep the door from hitting her in the back. The cart is filled with laundry stuffed into two Casper the Friendly Ghost pillowcases. The woman bangs the wheels of the cart down each step, lowering her tiny self behind it, one hand on the banister, the other gripping the cart. Casper smiles at the passersby.

Another car turns down, and Yolanda's on the alert again. This one is small, like a Volkswagen, and moving slowly. The car gets closer to us, slows down even more, pulls over near the barbershop. No one gets out. The driver is sort of young, maybe twenty-five, white. He looks at Yolanda, and she walks over to the window. He says something to her I can't hear, gives her money. Yolanda takes something out of her pocket, a brown bag, not very big. The car pulls away quickly, and Yolanda heads back up the block.

I work to catch up. She's excited now, charged up, like a winner. "We can do anything we want now," she says. She's practically skipping.

We reach Prospect Avenue again, and it's a little busier than it was before, more awake. We make a left and go only a block before Yolanda stops outside a candy store. It's got double doors made of dark wood, and looks as if it must have been a fancy place once. "Wait for me in here," she says. "Pick out anything you want."

"In here?" I've got a lot of questions for her, but she doesn't look ready to answer any.

"Right. Pick out whatever you want," she says.

"Where are you going?" I ask, a little scared to be left alone again.

"I'll be right back."

"To that place again?" I don't like the idea of her going there.

"You do your part, I'll do mine," she says, and then she's gone. She gets smaller and smaller as she quickly makes her way between the people in the street, and the shadows make it seem as if she's just like all the rest of them.

eight

A bell hanging from a string clangs as I open the door. Great. Let's let the entire store have a look at the lost orphaned white girl roaming the streets alone when she should be in school. But the only person who notices me is a man on the phone behind the counter by the cash register; he nods in my direction, but does-n't seem particularly surprised or interested. Another man, having coffee at the counter, doesn't even turn around.

The place smells great, of chocolate fudge and licorice. Practically everywhere you look there's candy. I walk along a long row of the packaged kind—Hershey bars and Raisinets, Nonpareils, Goobers, and Good & Plenty, and every gum you can name. At the end of the row is a tall glassed-in case of loose candies: licorice and gumdrops, jawbreakers, everything, even the red wax lips Owen likes. I wish Yolanda hadn't said to pick out anything, because now I'm dying for half the stuff behind the glass.

"Can I get you something, young lady?" The man is off the phone, calling to me.

"No. No, not yet. Thank you."

"Take your time," he says. The big man at the counter starts talking to him about President Kennedy. The man doing the talking has huge shoulders packed into his shirt and wide hands that make his coffee cup disappear. His clothes are dark blue, a uniform, and he's got a very dark face and a big voice. He doesn't care much for the president, doesn't trust "any of those rich boys." The candy store man doesn't say much, just "You got a point there" now and then. He doesn't seem to want to get into it, at least not with a paying customer.

I can't stand looking at the candy anymore, so I move to the back of the store. A few sparsely packed shelves offer stationery, pens, greeting cards, stuff like that. A lot of it looks pretty old, faded. The Halloween decals are more pink than orange. The biggest pumpkin is the very same one that's in the back of my classroom, right behind where Jimmy Byrne sits. Today is our math test, dividing fractions. I'm good at it. Jimmy always cheats off me. I let him. Why not? It's easy for me, hard for him. Might as well help somebody out. And he says hello to me now, too, even though his friends don't.

My throat is closing up; I'm going to cry. I miss my classroom, my desk, my view out the window into the school yard. I can see the seventh graders when they go outside for gym. The other kids have known each other since first grade. I can't believe I miss a place where I'm an outsider. I'm nobody to them, but at least I'm part of the class. My name comes after Mike McKenna on Mrs. Benson's class list. I was supposed to be there. Where am I supposed to be now?

I go back to the candy case and decide to count the jawbreakers in the fishbowl, but the bell tinkles and I hear the candy store man say Yolanda's name. He knows her, asks her about Cheryl. "She back yet?"

"No," Yolanda says.

The big man at the counter wants to know more. "She still trepsin' all over Mississippi? Stirrin' up trouble?"

"It's voter registration, Bill, voter registration," says candy man.

"Voter registration in some make-believe election? Tryin' to put a Negro in the governor's seat." He laughs out a mouthful of Danish, and grabs for a paper napkin.

"They're just trying to make a point," says the candy man, soft and calm.

"Tryin' to make trouble, you mean."

"It's the Freedom Vote," says Yolanda, her voice a little high, a little angry. "It's a practice election."

She's going to say more, but the candy man interrupts her. "They're trying to get people to understand the difference they can make if they was to vote for real."

"Them SNCC types ain't nothin' but trouble," the big man says. "Ain't happy till they wind up dead like that Medgar Evers character this past summer, shot walkin' up to his own front door. You think just 'cause Cheryl is young and pretty that's gonna make a bit of difference to 'em?"

"Luke, there ain't no point in—" the candy man begins.

"She just another Northern nigger agitator to them."

"You don't know what—" Yolanda starts to say, angry.

"Yolanda, come back here with me," says the candy man, calm but firm. "We got the candy cigarettes in yesterday. In the Camel packs."

Yolanda follows him and they come toward me, in the back, but her eyes stay on the big man, as if daring him to say one more thing.

"Where have you been lately? You haven't been in the store in a while," the candy man says.

"Had no money."

"You skipping your chores again?"

"I do 'em. Just don't do 'em good enough for Cas."

"Sounds to me like you're in trouble again." The candy man stops to straighten some boxes on a shelf.

"She's always mad at me," Yolanda says.

"Of course, you give her no reason to be mad, right?"

Yolanda shrugs, looks away. The candy man stops fussing with the shelves and looks down at Yolanda. His voice is soft; you can tell he's a nice man. "This is a bad time for you. I know that. But you got to look at things from Cas's point of view once in a while. It was never her idea to be taking care of a girl your age."

"I don't need anybody to take care of me."

"Talk sense, Yolanda," he says, his voice getting stern. "And remember, things are bad, but they're not as bad as they could be."

Yolanda rolls her eyes, but the candy man puts his hands on her shoulders, turns her toward him. "Want me to talk to Cas?" he says, more gently now.

"Won't do any good," Yolanda says, and pulls away angrily.

"I'll tell you what might do some good—if you tried controlling that temper of yours, and that tongue."

"No matter what I say to Cas she thinks I'm sassin' her."

"She's from another time, Yolanda. Another place. Where she grew up, no child spoke till they was spoken to."

"Well, this is 1963, and I have a right to speak my mind."

"And you have an obligation to mind your manners when you're a guest in someone's house."

"It's not her house. It's Aunt Cheryl's house. And it should have been my mama's house too."

"That's all past now, Yolanda."

"Well, it should have."

"Your grandma Lilly wanted your mother to go to school, just like Cheryl. She didn't want her girls getting married so young. That was the deal. If she'd gone to school, she would have had the house with Cheryl."

"Grandma Lilly didn't like my daddy. That's what Mama said."

"Your grandma Lilly wouldn't have liked any man who kept her girls from the road she had in mind for them. She wanted them to make something of themselves."

"Well, it isn't fair. People have a right to make their own choices."

"That's something you're going to have to get used to—things not being fair. Now, come back here and have a look at the new stuff I got in."

"You got the long licorice? The skinny kind?"

"Yup. And how about you, young lady?" the candy man says to me. "What can I get for you?"

I don't know what to say. I'm struck by the easy way he talks to me.

"She's Fiona. She's my friend," says Yolanda.

"Pleased to meet you, Fiona." He nods to me. And to Yolanda he says, "So, you here for another candy spree? You bought enough last time to keep a dentist busy for two years."

He takes a brown bag from the shelf behind him and snaps it open, slides the door open along the back of the display case, and points to his new Halloween candies. Yolanda agrees, but only to a few, then rapid-fire she pokes the glass with her knuckle and shows him what she wants. With each knock on the glass, the candy man moves to another box or bowl, takes up a scoop, and little candy waterfalls cascade into the bag, settling down inside with the others. Here and there Yolanda stops, her hand suspended above the glass, and looks at me, seeking my approval of the choice. The bag is more than half full. There has to be at least two dollars' worth of candy in it.

"Did I miss anything you want?" Yolanda says.

I can't imagine wanting more candy than is already in

that bag. But there is something else. I lift my hand, embarrassed, and point to the red wax lips.

"Them? You want them? The lips?" she says.

I nod. She raps on the glass. Owen likes them. It feels wrong to get all this candy and not get something for him. The candy man puts some in the bag; watching him, I get that feeling again, low in my belly, fear or sadness or something, because I won't see Owen today, and I don't know when I will see him. Owen and I fight a lot, and mostly I win, but not all the time anymore. He's getting big.

When my mother sent me downstairs to watch our stuff on the sidewalk, Owen was sitting on the floor in the living room with his bat and his glove. He had his hat and coat on, ready to leave. I was mad at him. Why couldn't *he* go down and watch the stupid furniture? But I knew why. He was just sitting there, his eyes fixed on the glove, his fingers tracing the laces. That's what Owen does when there's big trouble, starts counting the scratches on his fingers or something, waiting for the noise to go away, for someone to tell him what to do next, tell him when the coast is clear.

The candy man leads us back up the aisle of wrapped candies toward the front of the store, and Yolanda stops for Goobers and two Hershey bars. "You want any of this?" she says. I take the Nonpareils and some chocolate-covered caramels, and we head up front. The candy man moves behind the counter to ring us up at the register. A second man is at the counter now, a seat away from the big one. He studies his newspaper, doesn't seem in any hurry for the candy man to take his order.

"Who's this?" the big man says to Yolanda. I realize he means me, because he's looking at me, but it's the way you would look at something that has no insides, no feelings. His eyes are white and bulging, his black skin shiny and close-shaved. He looks mad at me.

Yolanda doesn't answer him. She's concentrating on her money, a compact roll of bills that she's taken from her coat pocket. Holding the dollars low at her side, so the candy man can't see, she peels away three of them. The candy comes to two dollars and sixty cents.

"You pickin' up strays now?" the big man says to Yolanda. She hears him this time, jerks her head his way. She's ready for something. A picture of how I must look flashes through my mind. I haven't combed my hair since the night before we got thrown out. I have Liam's socks on. They were all I could find yesterday, and they're loose around my ankles, black. I feel dirty. I must smell that way, too.

"I think I got something extra here for you two," the candy man says. Yolanda looks away from the man at the counter to see what the candy man means.

"Cheryl gonna teach this one to read, too? Maybe she oughta teach her how to use a comb." The big man chuckles, getting a kick out of himself. The quiet man glances over the top of his *New York Mirror* but says nothing.

"Look what I got here," says the candy man, a bit loudly. He holds up two packs of gum, with baseball cards inside, and slips them into our candy bag. "Mickey Mantle and Roger Maris," he says, and winks. "You a baseball fan, too, Fiona?" I shake my head yes to be polite. I'll save mine for Owen.

"Thank you, Mr. Dixon," Yolanda says, and takes the bag. She says good-bye to him and moves toward the door with me, but the big man starts again.

"You be sure to give my regards to your mama," he says. Yolanda stops dead, and I recognize that look of hers. "That's if you think you're going to be seeing her anytime soon," the big man finishes, laughing.

Yolanda turns, hands the candy bag to me, and moves without hesitation over to the big man's side. He looks down at her, smirking, as if he's going to be entertained. I don't see her hand move—only the coffee spreading across the counter and dripping onto his lap, the man jumping off the stool. He's cursing, slapping uselessly at his pants, trying to wipe the coffee away. Yolanda points her finger in his face, her other hand on her hip. "You are a nothing. You understand?"

"That's enough, Yolanda," the candy man says, still calm.

The big man is angry, flustered. "You little . . ."

"Sit down, Luke. Finish your toast," the candy man says to him. He's near the big man's place at the counter now, wiping up the spill with a wet cloth. "You're getting clumsy lately, Luke," the candy man says, but he doesn't sound as patient with the man as he did before.

Yolanda strides back to me and yanks the door open, disturbs the little bell. She steps outside with me, then stops and sticks her head back in. "And you don't know anything about SNCC or Evers or anything," she shouts.

She lets the door slam and looks at me, smiles and laughs her laugh, the one that lets you know that she's on top, that nothing can get her. She grabs the bag from me and takes my hand, and we run full tilt into the wind. The street is hers now, the day is hers, and I squeeze Yolanda's hand, pretending the day can't get me either.

nine

Loaded down with goodies, we head up Prospect Avenue, and I'm weightless with the joy of having them. A woman smiles at us—a little Puerto Rican lady with two little kids—maybe because our secret shows in our faces, in our step, in the way we sneak glimpses of ourselves in store windows. It doesn't seem to matter where we are. Only movement matters. The getting there. The knowing that we have it—all of it. All we want.

The movie theater comes into view, and that's where we stop. Yolanda pulls me into the deep wide recess that surrounds the ticket booth. The theater hasn't opened yet for the day, and the cold tiles outside the glass doors make the perfect place for us to plop down, to roll in our laughter, surrender to it. It takes us a long time to catch our breath and settle down.

"Did you see the expression on his face?" Yolanda

says, proud of herself. She leans back against the glass door, her face beaming.

"He was so mad," I say, laughing, and sit down next to her. I let myself relax, let the cool glass hold me up.

"He'll have more reason than that to be mad if he keeps pestering me." Yolanda sounds cocky. I love it. I want to thank her for not letting the man go on about me the way he was, but I'm afraid she'll say she didn't do it for me, that I had nothing to do with it. I don't want to hear her say that.

"Does he do that to you a lot?"

"Every time I go in, if he's there. And it seems like he's always got himself on that stool."

"How can you stand it?"

"Been wanting to tell him off for a long time." Yolanda spreads her legs wide to make an apron of her skirt. I do the same. She opens the bag, takes out the packaged candies from the top, and sprinkles the others out, like seed, onto our laps. We dig our hands into the deep piles just to feel the muchness of it, to claim it as ours.

"But you didn't?" I say.

"Didn't what?" Yolanda finds some wax lips and tosses them into my lap.

"Tell him off." I pop a Milk Dud into my mouth. The gooey sweetness enters every cavity, sticking to hidden places I didn't know I had.

" 'Cause of my mom. He helped her out one time. I'm not sure what it was all about, but Mama was always saying he was a nice man underneath, just had a rough way of talking."

"You don't think so?" The caramel coats my mouth as I start on the Nonpareils, confusing my brain about which taste to register.

"Nope. I don't buy it. I think he's nasty and angry on the inside, too."

"Angry at you?"

"No. I think he's angry at my mama," Yolanda says between chews.

"Why?" I slow the pace a little with candy kisses, unwrap one without tearing the foil. I pay attention to the smoothness, the taste, happy that all chocolate is not the same.

" 'Cause he's sweet on her. But she wasn't interested in him like that." Yolanda reaches into her coat pocket, brings out her money again, counts out four singles. "Here," she says. "Here's your share." She lets the money fall into my lap.

"What are you doing?" I say, grabbing the dollar bills so the wind won't get them.

"You're my partner. You get a share."

"But I didn't do anything."

"You risked getting into as much trouble as I did," she says plainly.

I don't know what to say to that, so I just say a quiet "thanks" and pick out another candy. I don't really notice the car, not at first, just a hint of color. We're set back from the street here, hidden slightly by the island of the cashier's booth. The traffic, what there is of it, sounds distant. But then it comes into clear view, coming closer. Moving slowly. A big bright, red thing. A brand-new

Chevy, newer and shinier than anything around here. The passenger window begins to sink slowly as the car gets nearer, and someone looks at me, at Yolanda. He's white. Blond. Young. I can't see the bottom of his face.

"You expecting somebody?" Yolanda says to me in a low voice. The car continues up the street, the window still half open, the eyes still on us.

"What do you mean?" I stop chewing, alert for whatever might be wrong.

"Family? Somebody?" The car moves out of sight; I hear it turn the corner.

I don't know what to say. I don't want to think about Mama, how angry she must be by now, worried. That's if Daddy had the courage to tell her I'm gone. But even if she were riding around looking for me, where would she get a fancy car like that? And why would she look for me in this neighborhood? I shake my head. "That's not my family."

"Pack up," Yolanda says, and starts tossing fistfuls of candy back into the bag.

"Why?" I say, confused, but too scared not to do as I'm told.

"He'll be back." Yolanda lifts her skirt and funnels the rest of her candy back into the bag, neat, efficient. I've already dropped most of mine onto the sidewalk, and I scoop it up in fistfuls, panicky. We hear a car again. "Forget the rest," Yolanda says, and jerks me to my feet.

We run in the direction we came from, and a car catches up, but it's not the same one. This one's old, a pickup; it pays us no mind. But we run even faster, seeing how little effort it takes for a car to close in. I hear the candy bouncing in the bag, Yolanda's quick breaths. The concrete hurts my feet, the hardness slows me down, making it difficult to move, like in a dream when you know you must run, when the only thing you want is to get away, to fly as fast as you can, but your legs, your whole body resists, as if you've lost your power over it, as if it belongs to someone else.

Yolanda is ahead of me, moving easily, alert. I hear a car again and look back over my shoulder. It's the red Chevy. Panic grips me, and I start to cry from fear. Yolanda slows down slightly, grabs my jacket and pulls me along. "Later you cry," she says, her words bursting out in short, raspy breaths. And I move with her, follow her like a dutiful caboose attached to its engine, with no power of its own, no choice.

ten

The candy man is washing dishes when we blast through the door and make his gentle bell go crazy. No one's at the counter, no one in the store except an old woman in a long gray coat, with a woolen bandanna tied under her pointy chin. She clucks her tongue at us on her way out.

"You haven't seen us," Yolanda tells the candy man before he can say a word, and she drags me down the aisle to the back, into a narrow place behind the stationery counter. She finds the door she's looking for, takes me through it and leaves it ajar.

The room isn't much more than a closet, full of shelves piled with dusty, discarded things: a broken coffeepot, lightbulbs, notepads, an extension cord, Christmas decorations, last year's display for the Miss Rheingold contest. We're both breathing hard, and I feel dizzy. It's very dark, but I can see Yolanda's profile against the strip of light from the door opening. She has her ear to it. The bell is silent and the candy man is humming. I try not to breathe so heavy, try not to move.

The tinkle of the bell announces someone, and I let out a brittle squeak. Yolanda drops the candy bag and presses her hand hard against my mouth. We hear footsteps on the wooden floor, then someone clearing his throat. Did he hear me, hear the candy fall? The candy man's voice says, "Good mornin'. What can I do for y'all?" He sounds different, more Southern, more colored than he did before.

The answer comes in a young man's raspy voice, but I can't make out the words. "Sorry. Can't help you there," the candy man tells him in the same funny way. More questions. More of the candy man's funny accent, then footsteps toward the back, toward us. Closer and closer. It can't be the candy man. It must be him, the kid from the car.

The footsteps stop. No one's talking out there. I'm afraid I'll wet myself. Yolanda's hand is hurting me, but I know if she takes it away, I'll cry. The steps are slow, close. Near the greeting cards, maybe, on the other side of the stationery. He's still again. Then we hear the scratch of a match, then a first, slow drag on a cigarette. "Tell you what," someone says. The voice is very close, very raspy. It's not the candy man. "If you see her, give me a call, okay?" The last words trail off as he moves to the front of the store again.

"Sho 'nuf," says the candy man, loud and high in that ridiculous drawl he didn't have this morning.

It gets quiet again, then the young voice says something, but we can't tell what. He talks for a while to the candy man. "Yo number, yes," says the candy man. "Most certainly. Most certainly. Be only too happy to help."

When the bell tinkles, Yolanda takes her hand away, and I realize that my teeth are hurting. "I'm sorry," I say.

"No matter," says Yolanda, bending to get the candy that has fallen out of the bag. "He's gone."

My eyes have grown accustomed to the semidarkness, and I can see kisses scattered here and there among the other candies, their silver wrappings reflecting the light from outside, like whitecaps in moonlight. As I bend to help Yolanda gather the candy, the little room fills with light. We look up and see the candy man in the doorway. He's looking down at us, and he doesn't look pleased.

eleven

As I take eager sips of the hot, strong tea the candy man has made us, lemony steam fills my nose. I've finally stopped trembling. Yolanda is next to me at the counter, and her legs look as if they're wrapped just as tightly around the pole of the stool as mine are. The candy man has left us to attend to a customer, and we stare at the small white candy bag the blond kid wrote his name on: Bill Donovan, in small black letters above a phone number.

While the candy man is out of earshot, we agree, Yolanda and me, on two things. One, we won't be calling Bill, and two, the candy man is holding something back. The first is my idea, the second Yolanda's. She thinks he doesn't want to scare us, so he's not telling us everything the guy said.

The candy man comes back, and Yolanda starts again. "He must have said more than that," she insists.

The candy man sighs. "Wants to talk. That's all he said." The Southern accent is gone.

"Which one of us is he out to get?"

"He didn't strike me as 'out to get' anyone. He says he just has to talk to you."

"You me or you her?" Yolanda asks.

"You both, I think," he says, and moves toward the other end of the counter.

"Why? About what?" Yolanda's bottom is off the seat as she leans herself across the counter to keep the candy man from escaping her questions.

"He said it's a family matter."

This is something new, and Yolanda pounces. "He said that? A family matter?"

"I'm pretty sure that's what he said." The candy man clears away some dishes on the counter, gives it a wipe, and returns to our end. He leans forward over the counter, turns a napkin holder around to check it. "Whose money are you spending today, Yolanda? Yours or Fiona's?"

"Some's mine. Some's Fiona's." Yolanda kicks me under the counter, I guess to make sure I don't contradict her.

"I thought Cheryl was suspending your allowance for a while. Isn't that what you said when I saw you last?" He turns away to get some napkins off the shelf.

"She changed her mind," Yolanda says. The candy man leans forward again to stuff the holder with napkins. "And I did some special things to get extra. Today I'm even delivering a doll for Cas."

The candy man finishes, then folds his arms and leans forward to look hard at Yolanda. "Listen here, girl. There's *some* special things that I better not find out you're even thinking about doing. You understand?" Yolanda doesn't answer, doesn't look at him, just swirls her spoon in the teacup. "There's nothing you can do in this neighborhood that I'm not going to find out about sooner or later."

Yolanda looks up but still says nothing.

"Now this Donovan boy," the candy man says, shooting a side glance at me, "is from up along Crotona Park. Is that where Fiona's from?"

"Mapes Avenue."

"Close enough. That boy looked to me like he's from one of the gangs that hang out near the park. They're a bad lot. And they don't like it much when they see Negroes and whites friendly together. Do you girls understand what I'm saying?"

I understand. My brother Liam knows kids in those gangs. They're always in trouble, stealing, fighting, especially with coloreds and Puerto Ricans. Liam is forbidden to hang out with them.

"I want you two to leave by the back door." Yolanda nods. "And if you see any sign of that car, you come straight back here. Or call me on the phone."

"Yes, sir," Yolanda says. The candy man moves away again to the other end of the counter and begins making a new pot of coffee for the early lunch crowd.

Yolanda gives me a quick look as if she's got it solved. "You ready?"

For what, I think, but don't ask. I've hardly stopped trembling, but I can see she's ready to move on to her next bit of excitement. She slides off the seat and slips on her coat. I take a last quick gulp of the tea and do the same. She calls thanks to the candy man and heads for the back of the store.

She leads me to a little anteroom along the back wall that has a door that leads outside. The door is a narrow, crooked, wooden thing with a bunch of glass panels and a yellowing shade pulled halfway down. The shade is crooked too. A rusty curtain rod is screwed into the top of the door, but no curtain hangs from it.

Yolanda undoes the lock, pulls aside the safety latch, and squeaks open the door. She looks both ways. No one. We step out into a yard no wider than the store, walled in by a patchwork of fences. The back is chain link; the right side, stockade. The left is a low, ranch-type thing, and the place has everything you'd need to start a junk-yard: old shelves, a rusting file cabinet, two or three old coffeepots, even a hubcap. Crates in the far right corner are filled with things that just don't want to fit inside: a broken stool, rolls of wallpaper, something that looks like part of a Santa Claus suit. Along the middle of the chain link, a long, low wooden table has half a dozen pots of mums on it. All orange. Beautiful.

Yolanda moves quickly to the lower fence and leaps over. I can't do that, I think. But I'm over in a jump and following Yolanda up and over still more fences, through yards filled with even more junk than the candy man's, through others with nothing but a broom leaning against a wall. Some have dogs, but Yolanda knows which ones and leaps back fences then, into the no-man's-land of scratchy bushes and mounds of leaves that separates the next street's yards from these.

Finally, we rest in a yard with a long red picnic table and a bench dotted with bird poop. A big red dog comes out to greet us, clumsy as an Irish setter but not as tall. Yolanda and I sit down, and he sniffs at the candy bag, so Yolanda digs inside to get him something. She makes him sit first, and he gives her his paw without her asking.

"What's his name?" I say, relieved to be off my feet.

"I don't know. I call him Jumpy. He can't sit still. Watch his tail."

She's right. It hardly ever stops moving, and when he whips you with it, it hurts.

"I think he weighs more than I do," Yolanda says.

That wouldn't take much, I think, but don't say so. "He's nice." I reach out to pet him, and Jumpy takes an interest in me, puts his head in my lap so I can pet the top of his head. He looks at me, then lets his eyes roll back as if he's been waiting all his life for me to do this. He's heavy, but I like it. So solid, kind. Yolanda calls the dog back to her, shakes the bag and gets him wild.

Our conversation with the candy man is running through my head. "Does Mr. Dixon know you do errands for Leon?" I finally ask. Yolanda tosses a candy in the air for Jumpy, and he catches it. His mouth makes a loud echo of a sound as it closes. The candy is down in a gulp.

"He doesn't like Leon," Yolanda says quietly.

"He doesn't know then?"

"It's not his business. Nobody's business but mine," Yolanda says, looking around for something. She reaches under the picnic table and comes up with a long plastic dog bone.

"You do it a lot?"

"Do what?" Yolanda teases Jumpy with the bone, shaking it, making it squeak. His big teeth suddenly latch on tight to one end of it, and he readies himself for a tug-of-war, rump in the air, front legs stiff.

"The errands for Leon," I say.

"Some."

"You could get in a lot of trouble." Yolanda doesn't say anything, so I go on. "Sounds like Mr. Dixon wouldn't like you doing it."

Yolanda pulls as hard as she can, but Jumpy defeats her easily and runs in circles with the bone, eager for another round. "Nope," she says. " 'Cept I don't do it that often."

"What do you do with all the money?"

"I don't get that much money." She teases Jumpy with the bone again.

"You got a lot today."

Yolanda's arms drop, and she looks at me as if she's tired of my questions. "The truth is I only did it once before, a long time ago. Leon was stuck. I promised my mama I'd never do it again. And I never did. Not till today."

I'm relieved, because the whole business is scary, and I'm sure it's connected to the Donovan kid. "Why'd you do it today?"

"I don't know." She swings her legs, seems embarrassed. "Seemed like we'd have a better time today if we had some money. I thought we could go to the movies later, maybe see *Cleopatra.*"

I'm surprised that she says this. I can't imagine anyone worrying or caring about me like that. "That sounds great. I haven't been to the movies in a long time, not since *What Ever Happened to Baby Jane?*" Yolanda looks pleased.

"Mr. Dixon seems like a nice man," I say.

"We've been going to his store since I was little. My mama had a job there once." Jumpy lays the bone at Yolanda's feet, and she plays with him again. "I think Donovan is from your family," she says.

"He's not related to me. We don't have any Donovans in my family."

"I didn't say *in* it; I said *from* it. Anyway, I know one thing: No white boy in a fine new car is going to spend time checking out some skinny little nigger kid."

"Don't talk that way." I don't like her to use that word.

"That's the way it is, girl." Yolanda stands up, holds a candy high above her head, but Jumpy gets it easily. She's not very tall.

"Unless maybe the kid did something she wasn't supposed to," I say carefully.

"What do you mean?"

I screw up my courage and say it. "Like something against the law."

Yolanda snorts. "That stuff for Leon this morning? White boys don't come around here to watch. They come to buy."

"Well, what else could it be?" I call Jumpy back to me, unwrap a chocolate kiss for him.

"I think they sent him out to find *you*." Yolanda puts the bag aside, like she's bored with it.

"I don't know any Donovans."

"You don't, but maybe your family does."

I shake my head. How can I explain this to her? My family would never tell anyone that I ran away. Everything that goes on in our house is a big secret. They'd just go around pretending everything was fine. "My family would never send anybody after me."

"Why not?"

I hesitate before saying anything. "'Cause I don't think me being gone is that big a deal. They've got too many other problems."

Yolanda laughs. "You think that. But it's probably not the way it is."

"I know how it is. It's a mess. My father can't stay sober long enough to notice anybody's gone anyway."

"You got a mother, don't you?" Her eyes are narrowed and the words sound like an accusation, as if I'm ungrateful.

"Mama's got plenty more to worry about than me. She doesn't even have a place anymore." I lie down along the bench, tuck my hands behind my head, and look up at the sky. I don't want Yolanda looking at me like that. "She's got enough trouble. She's better off without me."

"You think you're better off without her?"

"I didn't say that." I haven't thought about this before.

81

"How come you didn't go to her when you ran away?"

"I told you. She doesn't even have a place to live. And I didn't run away."

Yolanda gets up, walks around to my side of the picnic table, and stands above me. "What do you call it then?"

"I just decided I didn't have to go there if I didn't want to."

"But you know where she is?"

"At my aunt's house on Bathgate Avenue."

"So you could have gone there?"

"No. I couldn't," I say, my voice loud.

Yolanda looks down at me hard, stubborn, makes me feel as if I have to explain. "I just couldn't." I raise myself up to sit on the bench. "Why are you pushing at me like this?"

"I'm not pushing. You're acting like you have nobody when you do," she says, pointing her finger at me. "And I bet they're looking for you."

"Have somebody? What does that mean anyway?" I get up, move past her to the doghouse. It looks way too small for Jumpy, like it was built when he was a puppy and is useless to him now. I turn around and look at Yolanda. She just doesn't get it. She thinks my family is normal, does things the way normal people do.

"You think I'm some kind of prized possession? You think I'm from the *Father Knows Best* show or something? I'm just somebody they're stuck with. It doesn't mean anything to anybody," I say, and I kick Jumpy's empty food bowl across the length of the yard.

"Having somebody does so mean something," she says, and I can see she's angry at me. "Means you belong somewhere, means you count. Whatever you have with your mama it's sure better than getting dumped on somebody else's doorstep like you're some game they're tired of playing." She gives me a hurt look and sits down. Jumpy comes to her, but she won't give him anything, won't even touch him.

I stay quiet, not sure if it's okay to ask what I want to ask, but she looks all wrong there by herself, so small. So I walk over and sit down beside her. "You mean your mother?"

Yolanda looks away.

"She just left like that?" I say.

"Just like that." She says it slow, drags out each word, makes them sound like they're sizzling in a frying pan.

"She coming back?"

"I asked her that."

"What'd she say?"

Yolanda shrugs. "Said she couldn't promise anything."

"Maybe it's better that way."

She glares at me. "What's better about it?"

I look at the doghouse and think about how it feels to be me, someone my parents paid attention to only as a baby, before I got big enough to be one more burden, one more obligation to make their lives even harder.

"When I'm with my parents and they're fighting, it's like they don't even know I'm there. And even when they're not fighting, my mother's so caught up in how hard things are that I feel like it would be better for

83

everyone if I didn't exist. That's what it feels like when I'm with them. Like I should just disappear. Be gone."

"That why you're so quiet in school? You practicing your disappearing act?"

I laugh. "I do feel that way in school a lot of the time. Like I don't belong there either."

"How you feeling now?" Yolanda asks.

"What do you mean?"

"With me? How do you feel with me?"

It's so hard to know what I feel, so I tell her what I don't feel. "I don't feel alone."

"Yeah. Me too," she says. "That's something anyway."

We don't talk for a while, just play with the dog. I listen to a plane passing and wonder where it's headed.

"You going back tonight?" says Yolanda.

"Back?"

"To your father?"

"I can't. He's pretty crazy."

"What kind of crazy?"

"He might hurt me," I say.

"Looks to me like he's already done that."

I look away, thinking she doesn't understand.

"So what's different now?" she says.

"I mean hurt me physically. Like he does everybody else."

"You're afraid?"

I don't want to say it.

"You can stay with me."

I call the dog over. He puts his front paws in my lap and settles his big head down like he's been doing this with me all his life. I try to let the idea of staying at Yolanda's sink in. It seems so wrong, so right.

When my family says the things they say about colored people, I pretend to agree. But mostly I don't get it. In the South, they can't use the same public rest rooms as whites, and a lot of them are scared off from voting. You never see any colored people on television. It's as if everybody knows the reason for this except me. I just play along as if I do. Yolanda sounds different, looks different, acts different, even. But a lot of her feelings are the same as mine. At school, she gets mad about the same things I do.

If the rules still applied, the rules that my family goes by, this would be forbidden: to stay in a colored family's home, to have a colored girl as a friend even. I told Cait once that Yolanda was the only one I really liked to talk to at school. She looked at me as if I'd eaten grasshoppers for lunch. But there are no rules now. There's just me. Me and how *I* feel about it.

"Can I really stay with you?"

"We got the room," Yolanda says, as if that's the only thing that would stand in the way.

"Thank you," I say, but Yolanda doesn't take that as a yes.

"So you'll stay then?" She looks into my eyes, as if to make sure I'm not hiding anything there. Our run through the yards has taken most of her wiry hair out of the barrette in the back. It dances around her head, changing directions like dark shadows of New Year's streamers, and she looks like someone wild, someone magical. Her bright eyes size me up, like when we were choosing sides for basketball and she asked me if I could take Kathy Campbell. Kathy's five-eleven, but she never got past me.

"As long as you got the room," I say.

"We can take Jumpy home, too," Yolanda says. The dog leaps down from my lap, excited by the mention of his name.

"But he's not your dog."

Yolanda smiles. "That doesn't matter to him."

"He'll come with you?"

"What do you say, Jumpy? You coming with me?" The dog wags his tail and whines, as if the excitement is too much for him.

"He gets more goodies when he's with me."

"Won't they notice he's gone?"

"Sooner or later," she says, and laughs that laugh again, like there's nothing and no one she won't take on. Only this time, I'm laughing too.

twelve

Yolanda opens the front door with a different kind of movement this time, as if she owns the place, owns this moment. She strides across to the inside door and opens it wide. We follow her into the kitchen, Jumpy's nails tapping the floorboards. He seems to know the way. Something has filled the big room with great warm smells. Jumpy heads for the oven, and Yolanda opens it.

"She's got a bird in here," Yolanda says, then peeks about to see what else is cooking. "We're having yams, too." She seems to like the idea.

She grabs a metal pot from a low cupboard, fills it with water, and sets it down for Jumpy. He goes for it eagerly, wetting the tips of his ears and splashing the floor in a thirsty frenzy. Yolanda goes searching in another cabinet, finds what she wants, and holds it behind her back.

"Watch this," she says, and brings her secret out into

the open. When Jumpy sees the huge dog biscuit, he forgets about the pot and lunges for it. Yolanda scolds him, makes him sit, give his paw. He does these things in complete obedience, his eyes never leaving the biscuit. She doesn't make him suffer too long. "Good dog," she says, and gives him the prize. He plops down with it on the spot; his eyes roll up into their sockets in ecstasy.

Yolanda gets two bottles of Coke from the fridge, sticks their necks into the opener on the wall to get the caps off, and gives me one. Then she leads me back into the hall and up the stairs. Jumpy is right behind us, his biscuit in his mouth. At the top of the stairs, three doors open onto a small square landing, but Yolanda turns along the banister and takes me toward a little room at the front of the house. I hear Cas calling as Yolanda opens the door, "You don't have that dog in this house again, do you?"

"What dog?" Yolanda calls back, and hurries us into the little room. Jumpy leaps onto the bed, but Yolanda scolds him. "Not with that messy biscuit. Get down." He obeys and settles for the round woolen rug.

The room is very small, very neat. A white chenille spread flecked with holes covers a narrow bed. A dresser with a mirror stands on the other side of the room. Some knobs are missing from it, and the mirror has black spots. A lamp with a stained-glass shade sits on a small round table by the bed. Pretty. Next to it, a Nancy Drew book lies on some newspaper clippings. The headline of the one on top is about the killing of Medgar Evers. The curtains on the narrow window are the only things in the room that look new. They're ruffled and starched. Branches of the big maple tree touch the window.

Yolanda sits on the bed. I do the same. I feel awkward, and I think she does too. We reach down, pet the dog, say nothing. The wind comes up, brushing the branches against the pane, and Jumpy looks up at the noise as if to make certain things are as they should be. He seems satisfied and goes back to his biscuit. Finally, Yolanda looks at me, settles on what should happen next.

"You want to wash up? Change? I can give you something to wear." I quickly say yes, knowing I must be very unpleasant company by now. Yolanda gets a pair of dungarees and a blouse out of her bottom drawer. She motions me to stand and holds the pants against me. The legs end several inches above my ankles.

"No," she says, and drops the pants on the bed. "Let's get you something of Cheryl's. Come with me." Yolanda opens the door and steps out into the hall. Jumpy drops his bone and follows us, and Yolanda warns him to be quiet. We go back down the hall to the three bedroom doors, and Yolanda opens the middle one. The curtains are drawn, and the room is dark, smells like perfume. It's quite a bit larger than Yolanda's. The bed is bigger and has tall bedposts. Two photographs are framed on the wall near the door. One is a young colored man playing a trumpet. The other is Martin Luther King, the minister who's in the papers all the time. He's on his knees, praying with some other colored people on the steps of some big building.

Yolanda gets a pair of black slacks from a drawer and

holds them against me. "Yeah. That's better," she says. "We can roll them up a little."

"Whose are they?" I ask.

"Cheryl's. My aunt's. They'll droop a little 'cause you're so skinny, but we can belt 'em."

I want to know more about Cheryl, but Yolanda is busy about the clothes, looking in the dresser for a shirt. "You can use that comb," she says, pointing to the top of the dresser. I put the comb through my tangled hair. It's metal, but the teeth are very wide apart, so it doesn't hurt too much. A picture is centered on the dresser, a white ribbon tied to the corner of the frame: a woman in feathers and a shiny short black dress, like the ones they wore in the twenties. She's got her hand on her hip as if she's not going to wait a whole lot longer for the photographer to get the business over with.

"Who's that?" I ask. I want to pick it up but I don't.

Yolanda smiles. "Oh, that's Grandma Lilly." Yolanda pauses in her search, looks at the picture with me, as if it's the only thing in the room worth a second look.

"She's really something."

"Sure was," she says.

"Did she always dress like that? When was this taken?"

"I don't know the year. Maybe 1925, '26. Something like that. She was going dancing. She was always going dancing."

"Do you remember her?"

"I do. She only died two years ago. Sixth grade."

Yolanda finds what she wants, kicks the drawer shut.

"Let's go," she says, but I hang by the photo. When she sees I'm not coming, she returns to my side, picks up the frame. "This was her house," she tells me. "She left it to Cheryl. Said that way she wouldn't need no men."

"She didn't like men?"

Yolanda laughs. "Oh, she liked 'em fine. She married three of 'em. Just didn't like depending on 'em." I think about Mama and the idea makes a lot of sense.

"Your aunt's not married?"

"No. She's got no need to settle down. She went to college." Yolanda looks at me, and I can see she's proud of this. "Grandma Lilly took care of that, too. There's money for me when my turn comes. She told me."

I've understood for a long time that there isn't going to be any turn for me. Maybe this is what makes Yolanda so sure of herself. Not the money really, but the idea that somebody cared about her, planned for her. Like she was a person who counted, who had a future. I turn away; I don't want to look at the picture anymore. I don't want to think about Grandma Lilly. But Yolanda can't shake it off now. She wants to show me the old woman's room.

"You won't get in trouble, will you?" I ask.

"I never met anybody who worried more about trouble than you," she says. "It's a wonder you don't just curl up somewhere." It hurts to hear her say this, but I have to admit that it's crossed my mind. "Come on," she says.

The room is right next door. Yolanda opens the door slowly. The air is faintly stale, musty. This room is larger than the others, much brighter, with windows facing both the back and side of the house. This bed, too, has tall posts; a wide-brimmed hat with a long black sash rests on one of them. A very tall armoire with two doors almost touches the ceiling. A big oval mirror stands in the far corner, the old-fashioned kind, on a wooden stand. At the foot of the bed sits a little round cushion thing that looks like a bed for a cat. But I don't see any cat. Jumpy sniffs it, hoping he can scare one up.

"Do you have a cat?" I ask.

"They did for a while," Yolanda says. "Wouldn't stay once Lilly was gone. Just wasn't much interested in anybody else."

Yolanda crosses to the armoire, and the doors creak when she opens them. Inside something red and shiny breaks the darkness, and Yolanda reaches for it. It's the fanciest dress I've ever seen. Sequined, Yolanda calls it, and I remember hearing Mama joke about wanting to have a sequined dress someday to dance in. Yolanda holds it out toward me, as if I should take it, but I don't dare. "Here," she says, and pokes my shoulder with the end of the hanger. I don't move. "Come on, girl."

I take the hanger, hold it high. The dress hangs heavy from thin red straps, and I can see all the little round sequins layered one on top of the other, so close, each one threaded separately. When I look at Yolanda again she's holding out a black snake made of feathers that's got to be six feet long. "It's a feather boa," she says, draping it around her shoulders. I've seen them in the movies, but I didn't know what they were called. The thing changes her. She looks glorious, powerful.

"Want to play dress-up?" I don't realize what she

means until she takes out another dress, this one black with rows and rows of long shiny strings hanging from it. "You can have the red one. I like the black one; it goes wild when you move."

"That's the dress in the picture," I say.

Yolanda says yes and unbuttons her dress, lets it drop away. Startled, I watch her take off her panties too and step into the black dress, pulling it up carefully, getting her arms into the sleeves. "Zip me up," she says. I put the red dress on the bed and go over to her. The zipper is stiff, but I finally get it to start moving. The skin on her back is dark, just like all the rest of her. I don't know what I was expecting, maybe that parts of her would be lighter, like I am in the summer. The dress is big on her, but it still looks great. "Go ahead, put yours on," she says.

I'm embarrassed to undress in front of her. Ever since I started wearing a bra, I don't let Mama or Cait see me without clothes on. I feel different than I used to, ashamed or something. But Yolanda doesn't seem to notice me. She's busy putting on the radio and turning the knob to find a good station. I get my dress off and leave it on the floor where Yolanda left hers. I lift the red dress over my head, the way Mama says you're supposed to try on "good dresses," and let it slip down around me. It's heavy, feels cold and silky.

Yolanda looks at me, laughing. She's found Chubby Checker, and she's twisting her body around, making the dress go crazy. Jumpy leans forward on his front legs, ready to play, his rump raised, tail wagging. Yolanda comes to zip me up, but points at my bra straps, which are showing under the dress's thin shoulder strings. "Dancers didn't bother with underwear back then." I freeze at the suggestion. It must be a sin to go without underwear. It has to be. But maybe not here, just in this room, just with this special costume. Just me and Yolanda. "Come on," she says.

I hesitate, then reach back and unhook it, pull the straps down from each shoulder and take the bra off. Yolanda zips the dress up. The silky lining rests on my breasts, and I feel as if I've done something bad. Yolanda puts the boa around my shoulders. "Go see yourself," she says, but I feel nailed to the floor. "Go ahead," she says, and gives me a push. I go to the mirror, and it's as if I've lit up the room. Sunlight is bouncing off the dress from every direction. I can't believe it. I'm pretty. Really pretty.

Yolanda stands next to me in the mirror. Her dress touches her knees, but mine is short, just like Lilly's in the picture. Yolanda pulls one end of the boa around her shoulders, and tucks a piece under her chin. Her jaw is sharp, angular; she looks exotic, like somebody from a magazine. Her hair is wild, mine too, and we look as if we've been out all night. I try to imagine the places Lilly went to in these clothes, wondering if they were dark and smoky, like in the movies.

Yolanda starts to twist the dress again to Chubby Checker's song. The strings swing wild and fast. I twist with her, watching the red dress in the mirror. The silky lining moves against my skin. "Did they really go out with nothing underneath?" I ask Yolanda.

"Not a thing," she says.

I stop twisting for a moment, reach up under the dress for my panties. I pull them down and kick them away. Yolanda doubles over laughing, and I start twisting, twisting, twisting.

thirteen

"Has there been some kind of holiday declared that nobody told me about?" A woman speaks from the doorway. She's much taller than Yolanda, but with the same dark skin. She holds herself like Yolanda, too, as if she's got stuff about herself she's proud of, as if she's not going to tolerate any other view of things, either. This has to be Cheryl.

We stop dancing, and Yolanda answers her. "What are you doing home?"

"That's the question I'm asking *you*. You're supposed to be pushing a pencil across an arithmetic paper right now, not shaking the dust out of your grandma's clothes."

"We were sick."

"Well, you two are having one powerful recovery, I can see that."

Yolanda giggles softly at this, and I'm sure she's going

to make things worse. But Cheryl giggles, too, then closes the door behind her and comes in and sits on the bed. "Are you Fiona?" she says to me.

"Yes, ma'am."

"I'm not a ma'am. Call me Cheryl." She pets Jumpy behind his ear, doesn't seem terribly surprised to see him.

"Yes, ma'am. I mean . . ."

"That dress looks alive again on you," Cheryl says.

"She's almost as tall as Grandma Lilly," says Yolanda.

"Close."

"The dresses are great," I say, "the way they move, especially in the light."

"They're *made* for movin', honey, but not where it's light," Cheryl says with a wink.

We all laugh at this, and then Yolanda asks Cheryl why she's back so soon. "Did you get everybody registered that fast?"

"We're getting quite a few. But we're not finished."

"Then how come you're back?"

"We had some difficulties, that's all. Nothing for you to be worried about."

"You hurt?" Yolanda sounds worried.

"No. No. I'm okay."

"Then how come?"

"Never mind," she says, and goes to the radio to turn off Mick Jagger. "Now, let's settle matters about *you* being here today. It's bad enough for you to strut around in your grandmother's clothes instead of going to school, but putting ideas like that in someone else's head is another matter altogether."

My throat tightens. I want to help Yolanda out, tell Cheryl it was all my idea about not going to school, but I can't say it. I don't know what I'm afraid of. What difference does it make if this woman gets mad at me? But nothing will come out. I am the same coward I've always been.

"We were both pretty sick this morning," Yolanda tells her.

"Yolanda," Cheryl says, and sits back down on the bed. Her voice is low. "Don't go wasting my time with nonsense."

Yolanda lets this hang in the air for a second, making the accusation seem true. Then she comes right out with it, as if it isn't something that will send a grown-up straight into high gear.

"Fiona doesn't want to go home today."

"Why not?"

"Her old man's been drinking and getting crazy."

Cheryl nods, seems to accept this as if she's heard it before, many times, or at least stories much like it. She looks at me to see if it's true. She sees it is. "But why couldn't you go to school?" she says.

"Fiona doesn't go to my school."

"Then how do you know her?"

"We used to go to school together, the one I was at before I moved in with you. We were close. Right, Fiona?"

"From the start," I say. This is mostly the truth.

"Do you still go there, Fiona?" Cheryl asks.

"No. I moved to Mapes Avenue."

"That's a long way from here."

"I was at my father's. He's still on Bryant Avenue."

"And what about your mama? Does she know where you are?" It's all I can do to be honest but I shake my head no.

"Fiona doesn't know where *she* is either," Yolanda says in my defense.

"You mean your mama? You don't know where your mama is?"

"Not really." I figure this isn't actually a lie. My mother might not be at Aunt Maggie's right this minute.

Cheryl sighs, as if she's hearing a sad old story over again, and rises slowly from the bed. "You two better get washed and changed," she says with a glance at me. "Cas has that doll ready for you to take to Mrs. Carson."

"Oh, do we have to?" Yolanda whines.

"She's counting on you. You said you would."

"Can't you do it?"

"You made the promise, not me," Cheryl says. Yolanda blows some air past her lips and pouts. "Besides, I'm tired. I've done more walking in the past week than I've done all year."

"How come?" I say.

"We were registering voters for the Freedom Election in Mississippi. I work with SNCC."

"What's SNCC?"

"The Student Nonviolent Coordinating Committee," Yolanda says, pronouncing each word slowly and clearly as if it were something very important.

"It's a group that works with Negroes to help them understand their rights as citizens," Cheryl says.

"You going to give a lesson tonight?" says Yolanda.

Cheryl goes to the door and opens it. "No, we'll start again next week, like we planned." She pauses, then looks at Yolanda with some kind of grin. "See you later, alligator."

"After 'while, crocodile," Yolanda answers, a small smile playing on her lips. And though they don't hug or touch each other at all, I feel as if I've witnessed something very private.

fourteen

We're midway up the narrow flight of stairs that leads to Cas's little sewing room when Cheryl calls Yolanda back down. She wants to talk to her. Alone. Yolanda instructs me to go ahead, to tell Cas she'll be right up. I knock first, but too softly for Cas to hear over the machine's humming and her own. I knock again, and she calls out that it's open.

Cas is at her machine, hunched a little lower than this morning. I go to the side of the machine so she can see me. She does. "Fiona, well, how nice you come by. And you're lookin' fresh as a daisy."

I shrug, don't know what to say, but I believe she's really pleased, not pretending.

"This bonnet's givin' me trouble." I step closer and bend over to see. Under the needle is a delicate bonnet like you'd see on a Pilgrim, only pink. It would fit a doll with a head no larger than my fist. The sun rim is stiff and perfectly shaped; the material gathers around it in evenly spaced puckers. I can't imagine what she thinks is wrong. "It's perfect," I tell her.

"No, not yet," she says, and turns it around to show me the opening at the back, which she's trimming with white satin. She's skipped a stitch and the satin is loose in one little spot. Cas takes the bonnet out of the machine and gets a needle ready to fix it by hand. "Bonnets," she mumbles impatiently under her breath. "Who'd be dressin' a doll in a two-hundred-year-old thing that looked ridiculous even then?" She removes her glasses, rubs the spots they've left on the sides of her nose. She squints at me and sets the bonnet aside. "So you collect dolls yourself?"

I nod. She smiles. "I started collectin' when I was young," she says. "I wasn't collectin', really. They just come to belong to me, one after the other until there was quite a few. The first doll I got was before I can remember." She settles back into the chair, and her shoulders sink a bit. "Folks said I just wouldn't put it down, went everywhere with it. So people liked to give me dolls, 'cause I fussed over them so much."

She gets up, walks me across the room and points to a dark-faced doll in a faded white dress, tells me to reach up for it. I get it down from the shelf. "My mama taught me how to sew for 'em," Cas says. "I loved that. But not as much as I loved just havin' 'em." The doll looks colored; the face is made from a dark material. I hand Cas her doll, and she tells me she's had it since she was nine. I try to figure out how old the doll must be, keeping my hand at my side so I can count on my fingers.

"That makes her fifty-one," she says, and laughs. "You have a favorite of your own?"

"Catharine."

"This here's mine. Louise." She takes Louise over to her chair by the sewing machine and sits down, like she's in the mood to talk. I follow her and settle down on the wooden floor. "She's beautiful," I say. I want to say she looks colored, but I don't dare.

Cas pulls this way and that at the doll's dress, noticing things out of place that only she can see. "You talk to yours?"

I laugh. "Yes, I do," I admit.

"Louise knows all my secrets. Every one. These days she the only one wants to hear 'em."

"How'd you keep her so long?"

"I would never give her away," Cas says, misunderstanding my question.

"No. I mean all those years? Didn't you move and stuff?"

"I don't take kindly to movin'. Came up from North Carolina when I was a bride, seventeen. Stayed with my in-laws in New York City till we found our own place." Cas holds the doll out to me and I take it. "Came here seven years ago, when my husband, Aaron, passed on. Louise been with me every step. So's my others." She points to the dolls sitting across the top shelf.

"Did you know Grandma Lilly?" I can see the question takes her by surprise, because she looks at me strangely, as if she's wondering how I know her.

"I knew Lilly. Oh my, yes. Everybody knew Lilly." She

chuckles a little, like some memory is tickling her, and turns to her machine, opening the little place where the bobbin goes. "I knew her from when she started comin' uptown, to Harlem, where I lived. She liked to dance. Lord, that girl could dance." Cas's foot begins to tap, as if she hears some rhythm left over from that time.

"Did you go dancing with her?"

"No. No. My Aaron never took to dancin'. No. I made dolls for her. She found me when she went askin' around for somebody to make a doll for her new niece. So that's how she found me, and we stayed close from then on. Hand me that shoe box, honey." I turn to the place on the floor under the table where she's pointing, then reach for the box and give it to her.

"Was she your best friend?" I say.

Cas looks as if she hasn't thought about it that way before, then smiles at me. "I suppose she was. Yes. 'Cept she felt more like a sister. Know what I mean?" I can see by the way her face goes sad that there must have been something really special between them. She must miss Lilly badly.

"Yes. I have a sister," I tell her, but Cait doesn't feel close to me, not the kind of close I felt this afternoon in Jumpy's yard with Yolanda. "So you made dolls for Grandma Lilly?"

"I made dolls for the whole neighborhood," Cas says, searching the box of threads for the color she wants. "Christmastime I could hardly keep up."

"You're real good at it," I say.

"Well, thank you," she says, and smiles, and I think maybe it's okay to ask her one more thing.

"How come you're so mad at Yolanda?" She stops her searching, and looks at me surprised.

"You just full of questions, ain't you?" I don't say anything, and she looks at me with that look I've seen on grown-ups so many times, the look that says you've asked about something they think you'll never understand. She sighs and says softly, "Yolanda's goin' through a hard time right now. A hard time." She stops, looks as if she's getting upset. "My heart breaks for that child." She shakes her head then, as if to shake off the sadness, to see things straight. "But that girl's got a powerful anger inside and nowhere for it to go."

"Yolanda never hurts anybody unless they hurt her."

"She only hurtin' herself," Cas says softly.

"What do you mean?"

Cas sighs, goes back to her box of threads. "Ain't no point in goin' through life like the world owes you an apology, 'cause one thing's for sure: You ain't gonna get it." I think she's wrong, but I don't say it. I like the way Yolanda gets angry about things that are wrong, things that are unfair. When you do nothing, when you stay silent—the way we do with my father—it's like you're just as much a part of what's wrong.

I feel myself tense up, so I change the subject. "What do you do with all the doll clothes you make?"

Just then the door creaks open and Yolanda moves toward us briskly, taking over the room. But Cas doesn't seem to notice this. "Some I give away. The little ones that come to read take a likin' to 'em. I only have one great-grandchild. She'll be the one gets Louise."

"How come *I* don't get Louise?" says Yolanda.

"And when did you suddenly work up an interest in dolls?" The mood in the room changes, and Cas goes back to her machine.

"Could be worth something," says Yolanda.

Cas makes a disapproving face. "She ain't worth nothin' to nobody but me."

"She's beautiful," I say.

"I'd love to see your Catharine," Cas says.

"She doesn't have a dress like this."

"That thing's fadin' fast. I keep meanin' to make her a new one, but I'm always busy with somebody else's. Anyway, she wouldn't seem the same. Easy enough to make Catharine one, though, one just like that, 'specially if you're willin' to help."

I picture Catharine in white eyelet lace, a new hat. The idea is so exciting I feel weak again, homesick. But there isn't any home, and I push the feeling away. I get up and put the doll back, cross my arms over my chest. "I don't think so," I tell Cas. "I don't really bother with dolls much anymore."

"Why's that?" Cas says.

"Too big for 'em, I guess."

"Well, if you start feelin' young again and change your mind, you let me know."

"You want us to take the doll to Mrs. Carson for you?" asks Yolanda. The blond doll with the white apron is propped on a stand, ready to go.

"It's right here." Cas opens a drawer and takes out a big piece of brown wrapping paper. "I'm makin' a special dinner tonight to welcome Cheryl home. Don't you get caught up in none of Carson's nonsense and be late for the table." Cas carefully wraps the doll.

"No, ma'am. Not me," says Yolanda. Cas harrumphs, as if to say she's heard that before. "Fiona's going to eat with us tonight."

"Well, that's just fine," Cas says, and hands Yolanda the doll.

"Thank you," I say.

"Let's go," Yolanda tells me, and moves toward the door.

"And make sure that dog's not with you when you get back here."

"What dog?" Yolanda says, motioning with her elbow for me to open the door.

"You heard me."

"Can't move crooked around here," Yolanda mumbles.

"Hush up that mouth," Cas calls as we go down the stairs. "Your sass gonna get you into some serious trouble one of these days."

fifteen

Cheryl makes us wear hats this time because my hair is still wet and it's getting colder. Mrs. Carson lives only a few blocks away from Daddy's place, a long way off, so we sneak Jumpy back into his yard on the way, though he doesn't want to leave us. Yolanda is glad to let me carry the doll. She says delivering dolls makes her nervous. She's afraid she'll drop them.

We make our way up Boston Road, back toward streets I know better. I'm a little nervous about being seen around here. I hope the hat and the change of clothes disguise me enough.

Yolanda doesn't seem to notice, though. She tells me all about Mrs. Carson. She says she's crazy, but I can tell from the way she's describing her that it's the kind of crazy Yolanda likes.

"She knows stuff about everything. She's got a million books. She was a teacher."

"Not anymore?"

"She says they retired her. I don't think she was too wild about the idea."

"Is she old?"

"No older than Cas, but she doesn't dress old, just weird, and she doesn't think old either."

"How'd you meet her?"

"She came to talk to the Drama Club after school last year. Me and her hit it off right away. She says I've got a sense of adventure and that that's going to make a big difference in my life." Yolanda says this with pride.

Turns out Mrs. Carson lives in a big redbrick apartment house on the north side of Crotona Park, about fifteen blocks from Yolanda's house. She has a big skeleton taped to her door. Yolanda rings the bell and Mrs. Carson opens the door wide without even asking who's there. She's wearing a big flare robe that swings and billows every time she turns, which she seems to do a lot, like Loretta Young or something.

"Come in. Come in. Come. Come. Come," she says. She's got an accent like Dinah Shore, a singer my parents really like. When we get inside, spiders start dancing on my head. They're taped to the ceiling on long strings, just low enough to get me, though they can't reach Yolanda.

We follow Mrs. Carson into the living room, and Yolanda whispers something to me like "Guess she wants us to come in," but I don't laugh, don't want to be rude.

"Oh, you have it. You have it. Let me see. Let me see." Mrs. Carson doesn't ever seem to say anything once.

She takes the doll, puts it down on her plastic-covered couch. There's no room to put it anywhere else. The tables are covered in knickknacks. A lot of them are Halloween things, but most of them are figurines and candy dishes and odds and ends with ribbons and flowers and gold on all their edges. She takes the wrapping off carefully and when she gets to the doll, she lets out this sound, almost as if she's in pain, but she's not. She's thrilled.

"Oh, that Cas. That Cas. That Cas." She lifts the doll above her head like a priest consecrating the host. "That woman has outdone herself this time," she says.

Mrs. Carson turns, making her platinum curls swing wide, and looks directly at Yolanda. "I am truly delighted. You can be sure." She talks as if she's putting everyone's fears to rest, as if she were royalty or something, someone we'd never want to displease. "And I'm so glad you brought it yourself, Yolanda. I was very much looking forward to another visit. I've gotten some very special cookies."

Then she turns to me. I've never seen so much makeup on one face before in my life: two shades of eye shadow. Eyeliner out to her temples. The lashes are fake, gotta be, tops and bottoms. She bats them at me, and I get the feeling they weigh a ton. "And who, may I ask, is our new friend?" Her purple lips pucker out the word "new," as if they might suck me in.

"She's not new. She's my old friend, Fiona," Yolanda answers.

"Well," Mrs. Carson says, drawing the word out like it was six syllables long. "We have come to a new age, haven't we?" I don't know what she's talking about, and

I can't quite figure out the expression on her face. "Little by little, one small gesture at a time, we shall, indeed, see a new dawning, a time when little white children and little black children will play as one, will live as one." Oh, brother. Yolanda and I exchange a look. Now I get it. She's doing a Martin Luther King thing.

Mrs. Carson tucks the doll into the corner of her couch for safekeeping. "Come with me, girls. Come with me. We'll have our tea." She turns away from us with a swing of her robe, and the material makes some kind of swishing noise.

"What's that noise?" I say, hoping she won't hear me.

She stops in her tracks a little bit away from us and poses, looking at me over her shoulder. "Taffeta, dear. Taffeta."

Yolanda takes off her coat, so I do the same, and we follow Mrs. Carson into her dining room. The table is set for two and has a long lace cloth. The plates must be real china. They have gold on the edges, the cups too. Even the spoons are gold. "Take your places, ladies. Take your places. I'll set another right away." She gets what she needs from the china closet, puts the pieces down softly on the linen place mat. She disappears into the kitchen, and we break into giggles.

"Is she nutty, or what?" I whisper.

"As a fruitcake."

The room is very feminine, an unending kind of feminine. Ruffles and flowers and pastels are everywhere, on every surface. Everything matches everything else. Nothing has been left to chance.

"Does she always do this?" I whisper again.

"What?"

"Make tea?"

"In the summer she makes iced tea."

"What's the accent?"

"Richmond."

"Virginia?" I whisper.

Yolanda nods and mouths words at me. "Her husband's gone."

Mrs. Carson returns, interrupting the questions I have for Yolanda. "Well now. Our tea is ready and we can have a nice chat." She puts down the beautiful fat teapot, and I wonder what we're going to chat about. I'm not even sure I know what "chat" means, though I'm pretty sure some subjects are suitable for chatting and others aren't. There probably isn't much that Yolanda and I have done today that would be okay to bring up. And I don't dare ask her what happened to her husband and how she wound up in the Bronx, which is what I'd really like to know.

In the center of the table, Mrs. Carson has placed a three-tiered dish with cookies on every level, all arranged just so: long vanilla ones on the bottom plate, little round doughy ones on top, and assorted shapes in the middle. They don't look like they're supposed to be moved.

"Help yourselves," Mrs. Carson says. She pours our tea into the gold-rimmed cups and uncovers a matching sugar bowl filled with tiny cubes of sugar. She has a miniature golden spoon just for the cubes. The table is a decent size, and she's got Yolanda at one end, herself at the other, and me in the middle, so we do a lot of passing things back and forth.

Yolanda behaves as if this is all perfectly routine, answering questions about Cas's health and Cheryl's students, and about school and grades. I sit between them glancing left and right and left and right, listening to the china tinkle and the radio in the kitchen playing something by Tony Bennett and feeling like I've landed somewhere on the other side of the looking glass.

"Fiona, tell us all about yourself," Mrs. Carson says. She says it like I'm being introduced on a game show. I shrug.

"Now, we mustn't hang back. Shyness is not a virtue in a young lady. It's an encumbrance, dear. You'll do best to be rid of it. Speak right up. There's no better way to get what you want," she says, giving me a slow wink of her left eye. I watch the lid close heavily. Surely the lashes will tangle themselves together and she'll spend the rest of the tea party looking like some tipsy toastmaster. But the lid pops back, and her painted eyes catch me.

I say nothing, so she starts to fish. "Are you from the neighborhood, dear?"

"Not far."

"You go to school with Yolanda?" I notice that the cup in her hands trembles a little. She really is old.

"I used to."

"Oh, you're visiting then?"

"Sort of."

"Fiona's got a doll collection," says Yolanda.

"Fiona. That's an ancient Gaelic name," Mrs. Carson says.

"Gaelic?" I say.

"Irish."

"What's it mean?" says Yolanda.

"The fair one," Mrs. Carson says.

"You mean like pretty?" I say.

"More than pretty. Beautiful. Has no one ever told you the meaning of your name?"

I shrug. "I never asked."

Mrs. Carson looks at me funny—kind of sad—like some awful mistake has been made, something inexcusable.

"What does Yolanda mean?" I ask her.

"Well, I don't rightly know. But we can look it up when we've finished our tea." She must have her own encyclopedia, I think. But I didn't know you could look up the meanings of names in an encyclopedia.

"So you have a doll collection, Fiona? Is that right?"

"It's just a bunch of dolls," I tell her.

"Yes, well," Mrs. Carson says, and straightens her napkin.

"Do you collect dolls?" I ask.

"Me. Oh, heavens no. I haven't the room, as you can see. No. I give them away. I have six great-grandnieces. And there are many needy children during the holidays."

"You don't say," says Yolanda, and I kick her under the table, because I'm sure Mrs. Carson didn't mean anything by it. Yolanda takes the hint.

"Cas is going to show Fiona how to make doll clothes, give her lessons."

"How wonderful," Mrs. Carson says, but she's looking at me funny again, as if she's trying to narrow down what's wrong with me, as if she's almost got her finger on it, but can't quite place it. "You should be grateful, dear. It's fast becoming a lost art. Everything is store-bought these days, everything."

She looks from one of us to the other. Neither of us is doing much with the tea, and not a single cookie has been taken from the display rack. "Shall we go look up Yolanda's name?"

"Sure," I say.

Mrs. Carson gets up and beckons us to follow. We move out into the hall. At the end of it, we come to a large room with bookshelves on all the walls. Inside, a pretty couch faces the windows, with no plastic on it and lots of pillows in different shapes. We sit down, and Mrs. Carson goes to a shelf. She finds what she wants right away, turns in a swish of robe and brings it to us.

"Yolanda. Yolanda. Ah. Here we are. Lovely. It's Greek. It means flowers. Violets."

Nobody says anything for a second. Then I ask her, "What do violets look like?"

A look comes over Mrs. Carson's face, as if she's grieving or something. "Why, violets . . . they're beautiful, they're little purple—wait! I'll show you!" She goes back to her shelves, a different one this time, and brings down a huge book. She carries it over to us, handling it as if it were the Bible or something. She sits down between us, opens the book on her lap. She smells like a garden in the country.

The book is filled with big color pictures. When she finds the one she wants, she sighs and says, "Manet, girls, Manet," as if we're about to see something that will change our lives.

The thing she's fussing over is kind of plain as pictures go, just some purple flowers next to a letter and something else I don't recognize. I think they're on a table, but you can't really see the table. Everything looks a little fuzzy, a little out of focus.

"They're violets?" I say, and Mrs. Carson nods. They're really pretty. Now that I see the picture, I know I've seen violets before. But I didn't know that was their name.

Yolanda studies the picture as if she wants to memorize it. "Who's Manet?" she asks.

"The *t* is silent, dear. Edouard Manet. As if it ends in a long *a*. A French painter. A fascinating man. His work was shocking in its time."

The violets are pretty, but I don't see what's shocking about them.

"He was a man who painted life exactly as he saw it."

"What's the matter with that?" says Yolanda.

"There are those among us who do not wish to see the truth, who wish to pretend. Manet would not let them." Mrs. Carson turns to the book again. "This is one of my favorites. It's called *The Bunch of Violets*."

"That's all?" I say. "Just *The Bunch of Violets?*" You'd think a picture famous enough to be in a book would have a different name, something fancy.

"You'll find many great pictures named this way. It's of little importance, really, what such beauty is called. 'A rose by any other name,' as Shakespeare says." She shows us more. Beautiful pictures with simple names like *Seated Woman* and *Man with a Pipe*. My favorite is *Starry Night*. The stars are swirling, as if they're in motion. The whole picture looks as if it's in motion. The artist has a funny name, van Gogh. The way Mrs. Carson says it, it rhymes with sock.

I've heard the name before, just like the violets, but I didn't know this was what his pictures were like. Mrs. Carson tells us he was very troubled when he painted this picture. She sounds sad for him. She tells us little bits about all the artists, and I think it must be wonderful to know these things, to know a thing's name and what it means.

"It must have been hard to learn all this stuff," I say.

"Hard! Why, not a bit, dear. My father and I could talk for hours about these things—artists, their work, the times in which they lived. It was a pleasure."

"Was your father a teacher, too?"

"He never liked to think of himself as a teacher, but yes. That's what he was. A professor. An art historian. Taught at the University of Virginia, in Charlottesville. A wonderful man. These were his books," she says, gazing at the shelves, and her fingers trace the edge of the art book's binding as if it was sacred.

"Was your husband a professor?" Yolanda kicks my foot, but I ignore her.

"No, dear," Mrs. Carson says. Her back seems to stiffen a little and she closes the book. "Mr. Carson was an artist."

"You mean a painter?"

"Yes," she says, getting to her feet. She walks the book back to its place on the shelf. "His work never received the recognition it deserved, but he was a man of considerable talent nevertheless."

"Was he from Charlottesville, too?" I ask.

"No, Waynesboro, a place just outside of it."

"How did you come to the Bronx?"

Mrs. Carson goes to the window and moves the lacy curtain to look out. I can see the corner of the building that blocks most of her view of the park. "Mr. Carson felt strongly that we needed to be in New York, where his work would be taken seriously."

I want to, but I don't have the courage to ask her what happened to him. She stands at the window, her shoulders slouched now the tiniest bit, as if the memory of losing him keeps her from being as proud and confident as she was before. I can't help thinking that Mrs. Carson, too, is someone who loved someone who left her, like Yolanda's mom left Yolanda and like my father left us out of his life so he could drink. Different reasons, same hurt.

Mrs. Carson turns toward us. "Enough of that," she says. She moves swiftly back to her spot on the couch and takes a long look at my hair. "Would you think me intolerably rude," she says, "if I asked your permission to do something with your hair?"

I don't know what to say.

"Like what?" Yolanda says.

"It's lovely hair really, burnt red, the color of a leaf in

the autumn, but it's . . . it's all over the place. It needs to be . . . to be arranged. Yes, arranged."

"You want to *arrange* her hair?" Yolanda says.

"I'd be delighted to."

"What's wrong with her hair the way it is?"

"Nothing. It's just a question of taste, I suppose. It seems to me there's a lot more we might do with it."

"We could braid it," Yolanda says.

"No. No, Yolanda, I mean something a young lady might wear. What do you say, Fiona? Shall we?"

I shrug, though the whole business seems a little strange to me.

"Splendid. Splendid. We'll put it up in a French twist," Mrs. Carson says. She's as excited as a kid with a new toy. "Come with me, both of you."

I get up to follow, but Yolanda doesn't, so I stop. "Aren't you coming?" I say.

Yolanda looks angry. "Ain't *my* nappy hair she wants to play with."

"Let's forget this," I say, but Yolanda takes my arm and we follow Mrs. Carson into her bedroom. The room is one big rose riot. The chair is covered in baby pink ones, the bedspread's roses are bigger and darker, the ones in the carpet are red and mixed with huge green jungle leaves. It's hard to see where one thing ends and another begins. Vases filled with yellow roses are on all the dressers and tables. They're fake, I think, but they look very real. Even the vases have roses painted on them. And surrounding us on every wall, two ladies with big round hats and long, filmy dresses go walking through a rose garden over and over and over again.

Mrs. Carson sits me down at her dresser, and the mirror reflects the petals and vines behind us. I see Yolanda through the glass, looking all around. I guess she's never seen this room before. Mrs. Carson stands behind me and starts to brush my hair. I don't like it at first, don't like the hard bristles against my scalp, the sound of her silly robe every time she moves. Her perfume makes me feel as if the flowers have come alive to choke us. Every now and then her hand touches my neck or my temple and her skin feels very dry, warm.

"I'll need those pins," she says to Yolanda, but there's something in this that Yolanda doesn't like, because she ignores the request and turns away, plops into a chair. She puts one foot up onto the cushion, without bothering to take off her sneakers, and pulls the other leg tight against her chest.

I reach for the little glass box of hairpins close to the mirror. I hand them to Mrs. Carson one at a time, watching her hands in the mirror as she gestures for another and another. She talks us through every step, always stopping to brush again, keep the hair smooth. She talks as she works, telling us how her mother took care of her hair as a girl and how hair is done in the best salon in Richmond. Before long I feel sleepy, hypnotized by her voice, by the brush repeating and repeating against my scalp, tickling and tugging, until my head feels so heavy I can hardly keep from letting it fall back against her robe.

Yolanda says nothing through all this, and neither do I. It's clear the woman is talking mostly to me. Her eyes move from my hair to my face in the mirror, reminding me of the importance of every little step.

When Mrs. Carson is done, she picks up a hand mirror to hold behind my head so I can see how it looks. She's pleased with the whole business, smiling. It does look pretty, like something you see in the movies. I can't help smiling, too.

"What do you think?" I ask Yolanda.

"I think we gotta go," she says, and gets up from the chair.

"You look lovely, dear, truly lovely," Mrs. Carson says.

I look to Yolanda, hoping she will agree, but she has already moved out into the hall. I'm convinced now that Yolanda is mad at me, that she doesn't like me anymore for some reason. I get up to go after her, but in the corner of my eye I catch my reflection in the mirror. It's a reflection of someone new, someone pretty. I hear Mrs. Carson going on in the background about how lovely I look, and for a flash of a second I want to sit down again, to sit and be this pretty stranger in the glass just a little longer.

"You coming?" I hear Yolanda say. I come back down to earth, push the chair away and rush out into the hall.

Mrs. Carson follows us. "Well, I've certainly enjoyed our visit," she says. Yolanda is very quiet and very much in a hurry. She gets our coats from the living room while I follow Mrs. Carson into the entrance hall. She goes over to a little table where her pocketbook sits and reaches inside.

She gives Yolanda the money for the doll and says, "Of course, there's a little extra there for you, for both of you."

I say thank you, but Yolanda doesn't. She stuffs the money into her pocket and opens the door. Mrs. Carson trills her good-byes at me as I struggle into my coat. By the time I get outside to the street, Yolanda is halfway down the block, walking as fast as she can.

sixteen

"Yolanda, where are you going?" I call. "Wait up." The breeze feels cold on my neck without the warmth of my hair. The hat Cheryl gave me is in my pocket, but I don't want to put it on. It might mess up the twist. Yolanda is striding away, but it's not hard for me to catch up with her.

I walk beside her, sneaking glances at her as she stares fiercely ahead, taking the biggest steps she can manage. A boy on a bike approaches and crosses our path. I step aside, but Yolanda stays on her path, almost daring the biker to hit her. He swerves and curses back at us, but Yolanda doesn't acknowledge, doesn't even seem to hear him.

We get to Southern Boulevard and cross over. We're only about five blocks from Daddy's place now. Crazy Mary is on the corner, yelling at God. She's clutching a red umbrella with rhinestones in the handle, thrusting it out at the air as she makes her points, and people leave a wide berth as they pass her. Mama always avoided Mary's corner when we walked on Southern Boulevard. "The poor thing," she'd say, but I could tell she was afraid of her. When we would walk past her with Liam, he would talk to her and her eyes would brighten and she'd shout and get all excited and stirred up. We'd all giggle, and that didn't seem right, but I think it was better than treating her like an annoying dog.

After a ways we pass the dry cleaners and I see Karen Wilson and her mother coming out. Karen was in our class. I'm afraid she might see me, but she doesn't.

"Did you see who that was?" I whisper to Yolanda.

"Who?" she says, annoyed.

"Karen Wilson. That was Karen Wilson and her mom."

"So what?"

She's right, of course. So what. But it's making me really nervous now to be in this neighborhood at such a busy time of the day. We get to the corner of Southern Boulevard and 174th Street, and I realize that Yolanda is turning down the street, toward Daddy's place.

"You're going the wrong way," I tell her.

"No I'm not."

"What's going on, Yolanda?" I say. "You know this isn't the right direction."

"We're going to your place," she says, and keeps walking.

I stay right beside her. "What are you talking about?"

"Your father's place."

"We can't do that."

"You want your doll. We'll get your doll."

"It doesn't matter what I want. We can't go back there."

"You said we could get in without a key, right? Up the back stairs?"

"I'm not talking about whether we can get in or not, Yolanda."

"Didn't you say that's where your doll was?"

"Yes, that's—"

"Then that's where we have to go."

"No, Yolanda. Stop!" I grab her sleeve, pull hard. She doesn't like that, and glares at me, at my hand. I don't let go, and she has to stop. We're outside a butcher shop with a huge sign screaming about a sale on chuck steak, the same sign it's had in the window for as long as I can remember.

"Let go of me," Yolanda says.

"No."

"We have to," she says, less angry now. "I promised Cheryl I'd let your family know where you are. She's not going to let you stay if we don't. She'll start making phone calls."

"We can't go, and that's that," I tell her. Yolanda tries to pry my hand away, but she can't. For the first time I see that I may be stronger than she is. I don't want to make her mad, but I have to make her understand. "My father isn't somebody you play with, Yolanda. He's not some adventure. He's dangerous. He can hurt you, and he would."

"Let go of me." I do, mostly because of the terrible look on her face. "I'm not afraid. I'm not like you," she says.

The words hurt. If I had somewhere to go, I would run, curl up. I think of Mama, who always gives me permission to be weak, who expects nothing more from me.

"Do you want that doll?" she says.

I say nothing. It's a stupid question. What I want has nothing to do with anything. It never has. Things are the way they are. That's all.

"I told Cheryl I'd tell your family where you are. You can't come back home with me unless we do."

I look at her again. "Why are you mad at me?"

"I'm not mad."

"You are so. You're mad that I let Mrs. Carson fix my hair." Yolanda doesn't answer me. A woman comes out of the butcher shop, and for a moment I hear the ladies calling their orders over the counter, smell the awful odors, feel the coldness. I see the floor made of narrow wooden slats with spaces between them and wonder if that's where the worst of the smells come from. I move to the curb and lean on a big black Buick.

Yolanda doesn't join me. She pretends she's interested in something going on down the block, some Puerto Rican lady yelling at her kid for running out into the street. I wonder if the woman is saying the same things to her kid that my mother would say. The boy looks down, ashamed, so I figure she probably is.

Finally Yolanda comes alongside me and leans against the Buick. "It wasn't the hair," she says, crossing her arms in front of her, "not exactly."

"Then what?"

"Visiting Mrs. Carson was never like that before. That's all."

"Like what?"

Yolanda's voice goes up. "It was never about fixing somebody's hair or how somebody looks. We talk about the world, about books and stuff that counts. She reads to me from James Baldwin."

"Who's he?"

"A writer—a *Negro* writer." Yolanda says this as if she owns him, as if having this gives her something she needs. I shrug, but I can see this James Baldwin stuff is a big deal to her. I don't get what's so important about it. There are lots of Irish writers. Daddy says there are enough of them to fill stadiums. They don't make any difference to who I am or how I feel. But I can tell it's not like that for Yolanda. She soaks James Baldwin up like a dry sponge.

"So maybe today Mrs. Carson felt like doing something different," I say.

"It's not just that, and you know it," she says.

"No, I don't. I don't know what you're talking about."

Her voice gets high again. "You walk in with your Mick red hair and your skin all bright white and all of a sudden Mrs. Carson can't see me anymore. I might as well be invisible. People aren't doing that to me anymore. Understand? I won't let them."

Yolanda is so worked up she kicks the edge of the Buick's bumper, and it catches her leg, scraping her skin. She winces, bends forward, holding her leg, and I squat down to look at it. She's okay, but the scratch looks pretty raw. I glance around, trying to figure out the best place to go to get something to wash her leg. "Stay here," I tell her, deciding on the Laundromat. "I'll get something to clean you up."

"No," she says, pulling at my sleeve. "I don't need that. It's nothing." I don't argue, though she looks as if she's still hurting. "We've got to go to your dad's place, get that doll, let him know you're okay and where you'll be."

"You really think he's going to let me out with you again?" I say. Yolanda looks away. And I think it's because she knows what I mean. "You can get as angry as you want about the way people feel about the coloreds, but that's the way people are. There's nothing anybody can do to change it."

"That's not what I care about changing." She looks straight at me, hard, as if she's putting me to the test. Yolanda thinks she can be who she wants to be no matter what other people believe, thinks we can be friends no matter how other people feel about it. It's crazy, like pretending that I could be somebody normal, somebody special, when everybody knows my father's a drunk.

Her eyes are dark and pleading under her spiky black lashes. She really believes this. She has to go all the way with it, see my father. It's important to her. *I'm* important to her. I remember how alone I felt this morning, and my stomach tightens from the fear of having to give her up. I look back in the direction we came from, but there's no answer there, only a street full of strangers.

"Come on," she says, offering her hand to me. I take it and hold on tight. I lead her toward Daddy's apartment, praying desperately that he won't be there.

seventeen

But he is. I can feel it. He's there like a knot in my stomach, like the pinched feeling I get above my eyebrows when my headaches are as bad as they can be. He's there and he's waiting, not for me really, but for any excuse to let it all loose, all his hate and anger. Yolanda and I will do just fine today, I'm sure.

I take Yolanda directly into the alley, lined on both sides with curled brown leaves that will crack noisily if we step on them. I make sure I don't, and Yolanda does the same. We can't make a sound. I cross the yard, hoping Olsen won't see us. All we need is for her to spot a colored girl this close to where she lives. She'll be out with her witch's broom before we can make it back up the alley.

I reach the wooden stairs in a few steps and start to climb, then turn to look at Yolanda, thinking maybe I can get her to listen. It's no use. I can see she's enjoying this.

I grip the handrails so tight my fingers hurt; even my toes are curled. This happens whenever I'm near him. My whole body stiffens. I can't control it; it just does. I force my legs to take each step. At the top of the steps, I stop, listen. I know he can't be on the porch. We would have seen him from below. But he might be in the living room, just inside the door that connects it to the porch. He might have heard us already. He might be waiting there, knowing exactly where we are.

"What are you waiting for?" Yolanda whispers, and her voice seems like a shout. I'm sure he's heard us. He must have heard us. Yolanda pulls at the leg of my pants. I know I have to do something, but all I want to do is climb back over her and go down, get out of here, away from him. But Yolanda keeps pulling on my leg and I have to move on.

I push up the door in the floorboards. It creaks. I stop. If anyone were on the porch, I'd see their feet now. There's nothing, and I feel a silly relief, as if the danger is past. At least it gives me the courage I need to get the door open the rest of the way. It lands with a soft thud against the side of the house. I can't see any light from inside, not in any of the windows that line the porch.

In a few steps, Yolanda is with me by the door, waiting for me to open it. "Go on," she says. I turn the knob, but the door won't open. "Go on," she says again, losing patience. I press my shoulder against it, and the glass panes in the door make a shuddering sound as it finally gives, swinging wider than I'd intended. It opens only to stillness. He's not there. But the smell of him is there, the smell of cigarette smoke that shrouds him like a ghost. I step inside. Yolanda stays close.

The room looks the same—dark, bare. Pieces of Liam's broken 45s have been pushed into the corners. Yolanda looks at them, and her face changes. I wonder if she's thinking of what I told her about Daddy. She looks all around the room, her eyes wide and white. I turn on a lamp and move toward the kitchen, expecting she'll follow, but she doesn't. I turn to look at her. She doesn't look so sure of herself anymore. "Let's just go," I plead. "Please."

Yolanda doesn't answer. I grasp at the hope that she's ready to give up this stupid game, and in my mind's eye I'm running up that alley again, away from him, away from this place, heading somewhere else, nowhere, anywhere but here. Up on her toes, Yolanda whispers so close to my ear I can feel her lips moving, "Catharine. We can't leave her here."

I put my pocketbook down on the couch, and obey. To get to my room, we have to pass through the kitchen, pass his room. I take tiny stiff steps, my hands locked into fists. Yolanda is behind me; we're as close as two spoons. The door to his room is closed, but not all the way. I step up close, put my ear to the crack, listen as hard as I can. At first all I can hear is my own heart racing. Then there it is—his breathing, deep and phlegmy.

My legs are weak. I'm going to fall, I know I am. I have to get out of here. I look at Yolanda, desperate. But she takes my hand firmly, and we move away from the door, down to the next room, my room. We slip inside; I land on the bed, weak and panicky. To be in this place with someone else is like having a witness, like letting someone see what my life has really been like. And in her seeing it's become even more real, even more frightening. There is something about keeping things secret that protects me, numbs me. If no one knows, it can't be real; it can't really hurt so bad. In Yolanda's face I see my own terror. She may not understand it, but she knows it's there.

She bends over me, touches my shoulder. "We'll get Catharine. Then we'll go," she whispers.

Catharine is on the floor, her hat crushed where I stepped on it. Yolanda picks both up, and her dark hands remind me of Cas's, so gentle. She gives me Catharine and the broken hat, hoping, I think, that they will make me feel better. She sits down next to me, turns to the other dolls on the bed. "You want them, too?" I shake my head no.

"Come on. We might as well." She grabs Maureen, then Barbara and Betty.

"No, she stays," I say, meaning Betty. I take Miliscent and two more and we both get up and go to the door. We listen first. I take a deep breath and hold it. There's no sound, not even the breathing. We go out, past his door, which hasn't moved. In the living room, Yolanda stumbles on a boot and falls. Her fall makes little more than a gentle, thumping sound, but it seems to echo through the rooms. I bend down to help her get up. Her leg is bleeding this time, cut on a piece of record. I wipe some blood away with my sleeve. It's not so bad.

Then I hear it, his door opening. Yolanda hears it, too, takes my hand, squeezes it hard, so hard. Daddy shuffles the few short steps it takes to get to us and stands towering in the doorway, his eyes squinting, face blotched and ruddy. His mouth hangs open a little, and he shields his eyes from the lamplight, looking like some monster who's wandered into a land he doesn't know.

eighteen

I can't breathe. I can't think. All I can feel is this terrible tightness in my chest like a belt strapped around me. He stands there, taller than I've ever seen him, bigger. I'm scared, so much more scared of him than I've ever been before. Because there's no one else here to stand in his way. He has no one else to get but me. He sounds as if he's growling. He rubs his eyes from sleep, looks at us as if he can't figure out what he's seeing.

Yolanda stands up—jumps up really—and plants herself in front of me, her legs apart, her hair wild. "Don't you come near her," she says in a shrill, sure voice. "Don't you come one step closer. You understand me?"

"What?" Daddy mumbles. He sounds sleepy, confused. "Fiona? Fiona, come here to me."

"She's not coming anywhere near you."

"Where have you been? We've looked all over. Me and your mother have been walkin' the streets." He sounds angry now.

"See?" Yolanda whispers to me. Now she's sure of who Donovan is.

"Where have you been?" he says, and steps into the room.

Yolanda picks up the boot, holds it above her shoulder, ready to swing it or throw it or God knows what. "I said don't come any closer."

He doesn't seem to hear her or care about her. His eyes are glued to me, and he keeps coming. I move away, back toward the door, calling Yolanda to come. But she holds her ground. She's crazy. He's going to kill us.

He passes Yolanda without even a glance. In two strides, he reaches me and grips my arm. He bends over me, his face close, his breath stale, smoky.

"Yolanda, help me," I cry, and she does. She attacks from behind like a wild thing, yelping and jumping and beating him with the boot, beating his back, his legs, anyplace she can reach.

"Jesus, Mary, and Joseph," he says, letting go of me and holding his arms up to protect his face as he swings around to face her.

He bends over her, and I scream, "No, Daddy, no." Yolanda clocks him a few good ones in the head before he can get the boot away from her. She's still swinging at him with her fists when he stands up straight again and tosses the boot across the room. But he doesn't hit her, and I see now that he's sober.

"Calm yourself down. Calm yourself," he says. He's got hold of her arm.

"Yolanda, stop," I say. "He's not going to hurt us." Yolanda stops swinging, looks at me to see if I mean it. "It's okay."

"Let's calm down," he says, catching his raspy breath and rubbing the side of his head. He sits down in the middle of the couch, motions for us to join him. We don't move. "Suit yourselves," he says, "but hear me out." He smells of deep sleep and stale cigarettes, but the other smell isn't there, the drink smell.

We're quiet, and he rubs his head some more. "I feel like I'm in a Three Stooges movie," he says, and Yolanda looks at me, as if she's wondering if it's all right to laugh.

"Who's your partner?" he says to me.

"This is Yolanda," I tell him, still out of breath. "She's my friend."

"No question about that. And how do you do, Yolanda?"

"Just fine, thanks," Yolanda tells him, and it all sounds so mannerly, I want to giggle.

"Now," he says, getting down to business, "where did you take yourself off to?" His face gets serious, the way he looks when Liam starts trouble.

"I went to Yolanda's," I say, as if I'd had a plan all along. My voice trembles, but I can't control it.

"Without tellin' anyone? Without a call?"

"I didn't have much choice," I say.

He looks down at his bare feet. "It's no good runnin' away like that." He doesn't sound so angry now.

I don't answer, don't know what to say.

"And you've been with Yolanda all this time, at her house?"

"Almost all." If Daddy has any opinions about it, he's hiding them pretty good.

"She came by this morning early," says Yolanda, coming to my side.

"Where do you live?" he asks her.

"On Fox. Right off 163rd."

He rolls his eyes, and I know why, but I hope Yolanda doesn't. "Where did you spend the night, then?" he says to me, worried.

"I fell asleep on a bench."

"A bench?" he says, rising from the couch. His voice is loud again. "Ah. Bejesus," he says, and sits again. He rolls his eyes, rubs his palm across his face. "A bench. Are you all right?" he says. "What's happened to your hair?"

"I'm fine. Mrs. Carson—she's our friend—she put it in a French twist for me."

"You don't look the same," he says. He stops asking questions, and we stay quiet. "Yolanda," he says finally, "would you mind if me and Fiona talked private for a bit?"

Yolanda doesn't leave, just looks at me. "It's okay," I tell her. I know he never hurts anyone unless he's drunk.

Yolanda heads for the kitchen and leaves us alone.

He doesn't say anything for what seems like a long time. "I'm glad you're safe," he says finally. I don't answer, and the words hang there a long while. I don't know what to make of them. "Will you come sit by me?" he whispers, but I don't move. "Please?"

I don't want to be near him, but he asks again, and I see that for some reason it means something to him, for me to sit there by his side. He looks so different to me, so unsure of himself, and I realize that I can do this for him if I want to, this one small thing, even if I know it won't change anything.

I sit down on the couch, making sure we're not close enough to touch. He clears his throat. "We have to call your mother right away. And the police."

"Is Mama angry at me?"

"No. No. I caused this. You were scared out of your wits is all. Liam told me. He went out lookin' for ya alone." I picture Liam searching for me and feel as if I've done something very bad. "When he couldn't find you, he got scared and came back, woke me up. Never seen him so worked up. Seemed like he was even more upset than your mother about you bein' gone." Daddy rubs his hands against his face, and his rough palms scratch against his whiskers. He leaves his head in his hands.

It seems like a long time that we sit there, motionless, both of us hardly breathing, but suddenly, out of nowhere, comes a terrible sound, an awful thing, like an injured animal, like something trapped, trying to escape. Daddy's shoulders move funny, and I realize he must be crying. I reach my hand out to him, but I'm not sure what to do with it. I can't remember the last time I touched Daddy, or if I've ever touched him on purpose. I put my hand on his forearm, the place right below his rolled-up sleeve. His arm is very hard, and I'm scared of how strong he is.

He feels me touching him and lifts his head. But he doesn't look at me, just stares across the room. Finally, he reaches into his back pocket and gets a hankie out to wipe his face. I move my hand away, but he grabs it, puts it back where it was and leaves his hand on mine. It's very heavy, his hand, rough.

"Fiona, I'm sorry," he says. I don't know how to answer, don't know what he's expecting. "I know that don't mean much. But it's time I said it." He looks into my face now, as if he's memorized these words, as if he's determined to get them right.

"I'm gonna tell you something else, too. I said a prayer, made a deal. I said if He'd bring you back to us, I'd knock off the drinkin'. Knock it off altogether." He makes a gesture with his hand, as if it's final, all settled.

"And here you are, wouldn't you know." He grins, rubs his head where Yolanda hit him. "Just when I could use one." He laughs, but I don't think it's funny. "But I'm no welsher."

I don't know if I believe this, but I can see that he does. "We're gonna have a new start," he says.

"Sure, Daddy," I tell him, but I wish he wouldn't do things like this, twist my insides up with hope. It's easier to give up on him. That way I just feel all dull and hard inside. Thinking things will change makes me feel like I'm on the edge of a cliff.

"Come on," he says, and stands. "We'll go out and call your mother."

"Daddy, please don't call her yet. I'm going back to Yolanda's."

"That's . . . that's out of the question, Fiona. Your mother's—"

"Her family's having a turkey dinner tonight. They invited me to stay."

"What do you think your mother's goin' to say to that? Havin' dinner at some colored family's house?"

"Daddy, they're nice people. They have a nice place."

He stands up, as if to take control of something that's gotten out of hand. "That's out of the question . . . A colored family . . . in that neighborhood . . . You're askin' too much." I watch him take a few steps, gather up his socks and boots as if everything is settled, decided.

"I'm *not* asking. I'm going." The words are out before I can take them back. And I'm scared. I don't know what he'll do now. I only know I can't tell Yolanda I'm not going with her. I can't do that, not if I ever want her to like me again, not if I want to like myself. I stand up, and call Yolanda back in.

"Now, wait a minute . . . ," he says.

"Tell Mama I'll call her tonight," I say, picking up the dolls all strewn about. Miliscent's back is arched unnaturally, her arms in strange directions. I hurry to get her. "Tell her not to worry," I say. "She and Aunt Maggie can pick me up tonight if they want."

Yolanda helps me with the rest of the dolls and follows me to the front door. I open it, expecting Daddy to try to stop me, but he doesn't. He stands there in the middle of the room, barefoot, his hair in several directions, his face shadowy with stubble, looking stunned. "I'll talk to your mother," he says.

"Okay," I say, and he nods.

I move out into the hall, but Yolanda doesn't come. She's got something to say. "Sorry I did that to you on no account, sir."

"On no account?" he repeats. A smile starts, then fades. "I had a few comin'."

nineteen

Yolanda can hardly keep up with me, my stride is so long, so proud. Every little while, I look at Yolanda or catch a glimpse of the two of us in a store window, our arms filled with dolls. On Southern Boulevard, we draw looks and frowns from the people we pass. They're afraid of us, and I remember why, remember having the same fear. We make them uneasy, two girls whose skin doesn't match, armed to the teeth with everything it takes to make believe.

We come to Rollo's—a pawnshop—and stop to have a look in the window. There's a guitar in there, lots of watches, even a tuxedo. I spot our faces again in the glass. They're glowing. Is this what it looks like, I wonder, to know who you are, to know what you want and take it? Is that how I look when I'm not afraid? We move on, pass into the gray streets, filled with Spanish music, but the sky is just as blue, just as bright. I will remember this walk always, always.

We reach the house, and I'm eager to find Cas, show her Catharine. Maybe we can start the dress after dinner. If not, it will be fun just to plan it.

Yolanda moves up ahead of me to get the door, but it's open already. She stands very still, and I don't understand why she's waiting. She opens the door the rest of the way, takes tiny silent steps to get inside. She takes us through the porch this way till she can see the living room. I follow Yolanda so closely that I jab my chin into the back of her head when she stops dead in her tracks. She stays quiet, and I do the same.

I try to figure out what's different. I smell the same smells, hear the same groaning radiator. The chairs are just the way we left them, I think. But Yolanda senses something, something wrong, because she looks at me and shakes her head vigorously as if whatever I was about to do, whatever I was about to say must not happen now.

I look over her shoulder into the room; nothing looks different to me. Yolanda moves in slowly, carefully, like some street cat that takes no chances. She puts the dolls down on a chair. I do the same, making sure each one is upright. We can hear something upstairs; it sounds almost like furniture moving.

Yolanda heads back into the hall toward the kitchen. I stay close. Our sneakers make no sounds. She knows the creaks of every floorboard, which ones to skip, and I mimic her every move. I feel as if I haven't taken a breath since we stopped in the doorway.

We come to the kitchen, bright with sunlight. A small turkey has browned and lies cooling in a roasting pan that sits across two burners on the stove. I can hear something still simmering in the pan; steam rises gently around the plump legs, stretched wide apart, the gaping hole stuffed, the insides replaced with something new, something everyone likes better.

Yolanda crosses the room, moves closer to the stove. She has my hand; she's sweaty. Somehow this makes me much more frightened, and for the first time I can sense it, too, something bad. Something in the room is all wrong. Cas should be by the stove, or somewhere. I step on something. It's the handle of a wooden spoon, circled by spots of gravy. There's a hand towel, too. Where is she? Where's Cas? What's a towel doing on the floor?

I stand there, frozen, searching every corner of the room, every shadow. There's nothing. Yolanda nudges me, motions to the window. I take a step, look outside. Right below the window, in the shadows of the trees that line the long dirt driveway that runs along the side of the old house, is the bright red Chevy.

twenty

We hear the voices then. Guys. We can't make out every-thing they're saying, but words break through, some angry. "Nothing here," someone says.

"Keep lookin'," another one shouts, as if he's not in the same room with the other.

My heart is racing so furiously I feel weak. I need to sit down. Yolanda walks to the back door, panicky, pulls the string to lift the shade so she can look out. She motions me toward her, but I'm frozen in place. There's a lot of movement upstairs now, footsteps, furniture sliding, as if they're rushing, running out of time. There's no sign of Cas or Cheryl.

Then, without warning, the voices are on the stairs, ". . . damn kid probably sold it already."

"Neah. Probably don't even know what it is."

"Maybe not, but the nigger's no dummy."

I hold my breath, praying they'll leave by the front door and not find us here. Their steps are on the wooden floorboards, moving away from us, but before Yolanda can stop it, the ring hanging from the end of the shade string gets away from her and the shade snaps up violently, making a huge racket as it spins in place at the top of the door.

A small, sorrowful *oh* slips out of her and she looks at me. I can see how frightened she is. I think she might cry. There's a great stir then, as heavy footsteps come toward us, toward the kitchen. I feel dizzy, lost. They're in the doorway, two tall young men with leather coats and tight black chinos. One is in his early twenties, the other younger, blond. Their faces are not unkind—they could be anybody's brothers—but their eyes are angry and their lips are set in mean lines.

The blond one speaks. It's the raspy voice from the candy store, Donovan. "Where's the dope?" he says to me, but I don't know what he means.

"Where's my aunt? Where's Cas?" Yolanda screams.

"Keep your voice down," Donovan says.

"Where did they go?" she screams at him.

"Never mind them," the other one says. His voice is deeper, scarier. He talks like Daddy, like his parents weren't born here. "Where did you put the dope?" he says to me. I search my mind, desperate to figure out what he wants, how to please him.

"Just tell us where it is," says Donovan, looking at me as if I'm being stubborn.

"Where are they?" Yolanda screams again, and this

time she steps toward him, but I get to her first, put my arms full around her waist, and stop her from going any closer.

"Where is it?" Donovan says sternly.

"I don't know what you're talking about," I say. Yolanda twists and squirms in my arms.

"Your friend's tryin' to keep you out of trouble," the dark one says to Yolanda.

"What did you do to Cas?" Yolanda is wild now, kicking me, pulling at my hands.

"Shut her up," the mean one says, and in a stride Donovan is at us. He rips Yolanda away from me and puts a hand over her mouth, twists one of her arms behind her.

"Tell your friend to calm down," Donovan says to me. "We've been sittin' outside for two hours. The old lady finally took her shoppin' bag and went out. We ain't seen nobody else."

"Let go of her," I say. I want to do something, but I'm afraid of him. I don't want to get hurt like that. I don't want him to touch me. I can't keep myself from feeling relieved that it's Yolanda they're hurting and not me. And I'm so ashamed.

"You're startin' to get on my nerves," the dark one says to me, and comes closer. He leans over me and pokes a finger in my chest, hard. "That shit was mine. And I want it or I want the money. Now, where is it?" It's drugs he must be talking about. Yolanda must have his drugs.

"Yolanda, just do what they want," I yell at her. "Tell them what they want."

Yolanda stops squirming, gets still, but I know from the fierceness in her eyes that she hasn't given in. Donovan is fooled though; he loosens his hand from her mouth, and instantly, savagely, she bites into his fingers.

"Shit," he says hoarsely, and Yolanda slips away from his grasp. She runs, but it's useless. The dark one catches her, locks her in the same kind of grip. But this time, the hold is tighter, and I can see that he's hurting her much worse. His hand is tight across her mouth.

"You know somethin' you ain't tellin', eh?" Yolanda shakes her head no, and the mean one's face gets very red. "Tell me," he says, but she kicks backward at his shins. "Bitch," he says, and he does something to her arm, the one he's holding behind her back. Yolanda's eyes roll up in their sockets and some kind of sound comes from her, then fades.

"Make him stop," I scream at Donovan. "Make him stop."

"He'll stop when you tell us where the stuff is," he says.

"I don't know anything about any dope. She doesn't either."

Donovan looks at me, sees I'm crying. "She'd have told by now," Donovan says to the other one. "We gotta get out of here. They'll be walkin' in any second."

The mean one takes his hand off Yolanda's mouth and looks at his watch. Her head drops onto her chest. "Oh, God," I say. "Oh, God."

"Shut up," Donovan says. "Just shut up."

The dark one lets Yolanda go. She falls to the floor,

landing on her side like a rag doll. Donovan pauses, then steps over her. I think I hear him say to get her a doctor, just get her a doctor. Then he's gone and it's all quiet.

Yolanda isn't moving. Her eyes are closed, and her arms and legs are spread this way and that, all twisted, all wrong. Her left arm hangs behind her in a way it's not meant to. She looks as if she's dead. But she can't be. I know she can't.

I lower myself down beside her, put my hand over her nose and mouth to check for breath. Nothing comes. I look at her face, and terrible thoughts creep into the edges of my mind, but I push them away. I try again and stay still, very still, until finally, finally, I feel her breath on my skin. I leave my hand there just another little bit, let her breath tickle me, give the fears a chance to go away before I lean down and kiss the smooth dark skin above her eyebrow.

twenty-one

Cait tiptoes into the darkness of the bedroom we're sharing at Aunt Maggie's. She's holding a piece of Italian bread and a glass of chocolate milk and has my pocketbook over her shoulder. "You've got to eat something, Carrot," she says.

"No, I don't." I hardly look up. I'm on the bed near the window, leaning on the sill and watching the neighbor's daughter Gloria have a fight with her boyfriend. His arms flail as he speaks. When she talks, he looks away, as if whatever she has to say is pointless.

"Where'd you find that?" I say, pointing to my pocketbook.

"Daddy brought it over," she says, and hands it to me. "You left it at his place."

"Oh, right. That's where I had it last." I look to see how Gloria is doing. Her boyfriend has turned his back on her.

"You really did it this time," Cait says. She puts the glass and plate down on the nightstand and sits down on the other twin bed. "Mama was mad enough when she didn't know where you were. You should have left it like that. Least that way she was mostly mad at Daddy."

"I tried to. Daddy told her."

"That's 'cause he was so scared about you." Cait has that look on her face, the one that says "He likes you best."

I decide to ignore it. "Is Mama still going on about everything?"

"Not as much," Cait says, and sips the milk.

"Do you think he's really going to stop?" I ask her.

"Stop what?"

"Drinking."

She rolls her eyes and wipes her mouth with the back of her hand. "They're going on about it in there like it's his first pledge."

"Maybe this is different."

"Why? 'Cause he almost lost his precious?"

"Oh, stop it."

She takes a diaper from the stack near the crib and throws it at my head, but I deflect it. "You're the only one he doesn't knock around," she says.

I turn back to the window. I don't want to think about Daddy. I don't want to be here, stuck in my baby cousin's bedroom, with his crib and his stuffed animals and the smell of diapers. I want to be with Yolanda.

Mama headed out to get me as soon as Daddy told her where I was. "I've come to get my daughter" was all she said. She didn't say "... out of this snakepit." That part she reserved for the expression on her face.

She arrived just as they were putting Yolanda into the ambulance. Cas had returned by then, too, dropping her bag of groceries at the sight of us. I was afraid to tell Cas what the boys had been looking for, afraid I might get Yolanda into trouble. Cas wasn't happy with my explanation, but at least I could tell her that I'd had the good sense to call an ambulance.

Mama wouldn't let me go into the ambulance with Yolanda no matter how much I pleaded. "You go on with your mother," Cas finally said. "Yolanda will be all right." I hope she wasn't just saying that to make me stop crying.

Once we got into Aunt Maggie's car, Mama let loose. How worried she'd been. What a terrible neighborhood this was. The "element" that lived here and what went on in these houses. She didn't say anything about what went on in our house, so I figured that subject was off-limits. She just went on about "these people," saying they were "the lowest of the low" and had no respect for themselves or concern for anyone else. How I was or how I felt about Yolanda or what had just happened to her never came up.

"Are you going to eat?" Cait says.

"I don't want to eat," I say, and watch Gloria try again to get her boyfriend to listen. She's tugging at his sleeve now.

"Do you want me to bring you something else?" Cait says.

"I just want to see Yolanda."

Cait shakes her head like I'm a lost cause and gets up from the bed. She closes the door behind her, and I'm alone, feeling that feeling again, the one that came over me in the car on the way here. I don't have a name for it, and it's very hard to describe, but it makes me feel different, act different, from before.

In the car, Mama had gone on about all the grief I'd caused everyone, how worried they all were, until finally—as if these mortal sins were too big to speak of anymore—she settled on my hair. Who had done that to my hair, she wanted to know. I hadn't let that colored girl touch my hair, had I? I didn't answer. I hadn't said a thing to her the whole ride. But finally I heard her say, "Can you believe it, Maggie, letting that one play with her hair?" and I pictured Yolanda's dark hands pouring my cereal, pulling me up the street, handing me Catharine. "She looks ridiculous, like a forty-year-old woman."

Then I did it. I said it. "I like it." Something I know I never would have said before.

"Say that again," Mama said. The look on her face was pure shock. I was on the side of her bad ear, and her question brought that night back, his hand swinging, her tears, and I saw clearly what's wrong with us. Living with Daddy has done something bad not just to Mama but to both of us, made us grow out of shape, like plants that can't get to the light. I knew she'd be angry, knew that it wasn't the kind of answer she needed from me right then, or the kind she's come to expect, but I said it again. "I like it." And I made sure she heard me, made sure she knew

154

that this time I wouldn't pretend for her that I was bad and wrong for having an opinion of my own.

Commands drift in from down the hall. Aunt Maggie is telling her older ones to get ready for their bath. It'll be time for bed soon. I feel tired, too, and let myself yawn. I see my reflection in the windowpane that frames the night and reach around to touch the smoothness of my twist again. Gloria is by herself now, leaning on the mailbox, dabbing her eyes with the edge of her sleeve in that funny way girls do when they don't want to mess their mascara. After a while I start to pull the shiny hairpins out one at a time, so many, until finally my hair loosens and falls around my face. I'm starting to feel like my old self again, and that scares me, but somehow I know that I'm not that person anymore.

twenty-two

Mama is at the kitchen table by the window reading the *New York Mirror*. She's already finished the *Daily News* and put it aside. She loves to get up early on Saturdays and Sundays and read the papers, relax for an hour. Aunt Maggie knows it, too. That's probably why she went out to the store so early. Everybody else in the house is sleeping.

Usually, when Mama reads, I hang out close by and she tells me what's going on in the world. Most of it's not very good, but it's fun to hear.

I love the murder cases. If a woman's been molested or something, Mama will leave that part out, so I read it later for myself. I love when there's stuff about movie stars. Mama likes the stories about City Hall and the crooked politicians, but to me those stories sound like the same ones over and over, only with different names. Rescues are my favorites, especially fires.

I ask Mama if it's all right to get myself some juice. She says I can, says Aunt Maggie told her we should feel right at home. But it doesn't feel like home. It feels awful, like I'm grubbing somebody's food. A place can't be *like* home; it's either home or it isn't. And when it isn't, you know it. No matter what anyone says, you know you don't belong.

"I'll make you some breakfast," Mama says, and starts to get up. "We have a little pancake mix."

"No, I'm not hungry," I tell her. I don't want to spoil her time with the papers.

Mama picks up the *Mirror* again, and I sit across from her at the table with my orange juice. I watch her giant eyes through her reading glasses as they scan the page and finally settle on something.

"That nonsense is still goin' on down there," she says, and clucks her tongue.

"Down where?"

"Mississippi. They're puttin' a Negro up for governor. Some guy named Aaron Henry with the Mississippi Freedom Democratic Party. They're doin' it just to rile things up." Just what I need. A story about Negroes. "He's not really even on the ballot. They just want to show how many coloreds they could get out to vote if they wanted to. That's all Communists behind that. Mark my words."

I had this crazy idea as I went to sleep last night that if I kept her mind off Yolanda being colored, she'd forget about it. Like I did. That way she wouldn't put up such a fuss when I ask her if I can go visit Yolanda at the hospital.

I don't say anything about Mississippi. I turn to the

window. It's bright outside. The windowpane feels warm already from the sun. The leaves in the yard have been swept into bright mounds. A cat, mostly black, darts by one of them, sends leaves flying. I think about Jumpy, about our trek through the yards. Once during the walk back, Yolanda asked me what I want to be when I grow up. A teacher, I told her, but what I really want to be is a singer. I asked her what she wants to be and she said a lawyer. I've never heard of a girl lawyer before, never mind a colored one, so I said something really stupid. "You're going to go to school to be a colored lawyer?"

"I'm just going to study to be a lawyer. The colored part I already got down pat." I laughed, but she didn't. She just told me about all the things she was going to fight for in court. The right to do this, the right to do that. She went on for a while, long past when I stopped listening. It's not that I wasn't interested. I just couldn't get past the colored part and that she was a girl. I've seen only one or two colored lawyers in the papers or on TV, and none of them were girls. I saw a movie once where Katharine Hepburn played a lawyer, but that's in the movies.

At first, I thought Yolanda hadn't noticed any of this—the way things are in real life. But the more I listened to her, the more I understood the real difference between Yolanda and me. She *has* noticed it. All of it. She knows that's not what other colored girls do. She just isn't going to let it stop her, the way it would stop me.

Mama's voice breaks in. "How're you feeling, Fiona?"

"I'm fine," I tell her, and decide to dive in. "Mama," I

say softly as she gets up to make another pot of coffee. "Mama," I say again. She doesn't answer me. She takes the lid off the pot to get rid of the old grinds.

I speak a little louder. "Mama, I want to go to see Yolanda today."

"What?" she says, as if I'm some annoying radio static that she can't tune out.

I say it again, louder. "Mama, I want to go to see Yolanda today." But I know she heard me the first time; I can tell from the expression on her face, the look I'm getting.

She starts out mildly enough. "That wouldn't be right. That's for her family to do." She turns away from me. I'm sure she thinks I'll say no more about it. Part of me understands what she's saying, agrees with it almost. But only because that's the way things have always been. I never thought about it before. Now I am thinking about it, and none of it makes sense.

"She's my friend," I say, flipping the pages of the paper, deciding to play it just as casually. "I want to go see her."

"You can make a card and send it to her. We'll put it in the mail today. She'll have it in a day or so." She goes back to her coffee-making as if everything is settled.

This angers me, her acting as if what I want is so easy to put aside. "No. I need to see her."

"That's impossible." She looks at me as if I'm some dolt who hasn't learned the rules yet. "You don't need to see her."

"I know what I need, Mama. Please don't tell me what I need." I feel my face getting hot, my stomach

159

tightening up. Being angry is not allowed with my mother. Only she's allowed to be angry.

"I'm your mother. It's my job to know what you need." She points a measuring spoon at me like it's a gavel. "And the last thing you need is to get involved with a family like that." I lower my eyes to the paper.

It's all I can do to keep from groaning, but I know it would hurt her. Mama has this pride that she's raised us against all odds, with no help from Daddy, and that none of us has ever gotten into any serious trouble. "It's a good family," I say, more to the paper than to her.

"What do her parents do?"

"She has no parents."

"She has no father and no mother and you call that a family?" I look up. Mama's got her hands on her hips, as if everything right and good is on her side. And all at once I'm so sick of her, sick of her deciding everything as if she really knew any better, had any more understanding of things than I do.

"Do I have a father?" I say.

"You certainly do, young lady. And don't you ever let me hear you say a word against him."

"What about the drinking?"

"Your father's drinkin' is my problem, not yours."

"It's not mine?" I say, jumping up from the table, and my skin gets goose bumps from the shock of answering her back this way. "Not Owen's? Not Liam's? What about Cait? She has to do all the housework so you can work. Whose problem is that?"

"What's gotten into you?" She says this like she's talking to a madwoman.

"I don't get it."

She waits for more, but I just stare at her.

"Get what?" she says finally.

"Why everything comes back to the honor-thy-mother-and-father thing. What's honor mean anyway?" The look on her face tells me I've turned into a stranger.

"I can't believe I'm hearing this," she says.

"When is it our turn to get honored? At least Yolanda treats me like a person, like I count."

"Just who do you think you're talkin' to?"

"I just want to see Yolanda."

Liam shuffles into the kitchen, solemn, without greeting us. He must have been out late, because he wasn't around when I got here last night. He nods at me and opens the fridge.

"Forget about this Yolanda. You're not going to see her," Mama says. Her voice is trembling, on the verge of a scream. "I don't want to hear any more about Yolanda." She says her name as if it's some strange, foreign thing, something she can feel free to mock. I think of the way Mrs. Carson said our names, as if they were jewels, things to be proud of, admired. Mama runs water into the coffeepot; Liam coughs. The kitchen gets quiet.

I sit down again, swallow hard. "Yes, I am," I say.

"What did you say?" Mama slams something down.

"She's my friend. I have a right to go see her."

"A right? Listen to her," Mama says to Liam. "She's startin' to *talk* like one of 'em."

Liam doesn't answer her. He sits down at the table, puts the *Daily News* in front of him, opens a bottle of Coke.

"How you doin', wanderer?" he says to me.

"I'm okay."

He takes my word for it and gives his attention to the paper. His face is pretty scratched up. I remember the records breaking, the shame of leaving him there, all of it. I don't want that feeling ever again. Not doing what you know you should do, what you know is right to do. It's like giving part of yourself away, a part that should belong only to you.

"Liam, what bus goes to Lincoln Hospital from here?" I ask him.

"Number three will take you there. You can walk up to Southern Boulevard and get it. That's the best way."

"And how do you think you're goin' to get bus fare?" Mama says.

I don't tell Mama about the money Yolanda gave me. "I can spot you a quarter," Liam says.

"I want no more of this talk." Mama's voice is loud now. "You understand me?"

"No," I say, "I don't. I don't understand you."

"I said no, and that's final."

"She wants to see her friend," says Liam. "What's the big deal?"

"Her 'friend,'" Mama says, dragging the word out, abusing it, "happens to be a nigger."

"So what?" Liam says.

"Listen, you two, I decide who goes where around here."

"You're startin' to lose track lately," he says, and takes a swig of soda.

"That's enough out of you," Mama says.

I stand up. I don't want Liam fighting my battles for me, especially not this one. I leave them in the kitchen, go out into the hall that leads to the front door. Mama is calling me, but I don't answer. Cheryl's jacket is on the rack with all the others. I take it and go back into the kitchen.

For a time I stand there in the doorway. I don't know what to say. Mama seems frozen in place, a dish towel in her hand. "You're goin' then?"

"I'm going." I force myself to enter the room, go to her. I give her a kiss on the cheek, the same way I would no matter where I was going, no matter who I was going to see. Her skin is cool, loose. She looks older this morning, without her makeup. Up close I can smell the face cream she uses. "I have to, Mama," I whisper, and turn away.

She grabs my forearm, looks at me. I look back into her eyes; they're watery. I don't want to hurt her. She doesn't need any more hurts. "It's not safe," she says. "Whatever's goin' on in that family, it's not safe."

"I'll be all right," I tell her, the same thing we all tell her when she has to leave us alone, or leave us with Daddy, because that's what she needs to hear. That's what she needs to believe. She grips my hand tight. I know she can't bear the thought of anything happening to me. She has no place for that. She can handle all the rest of the mess life gives her, but she couldn't handle that.

I pull away, and she loosens her grasp, lets me go. I take my pocketbook from the corner and go out into the hall, then walk with my head down along the long hall to the front door and open it without looking up. But the day is beautiful, warm. The air smells fresh, like it's brand-new, like they brought it in from the country somewhere. I decide to walk up to the boulevard, get a bus from there. I take big strides, breathe deep. I keep my face to the sky, watch a cloud float in, and for a crazy second it seems as if his voice is coming from there, from the sky.

"Fiona. Hey, Fiona, wait up."

twenty-three

I stop, turn. Liam is a half a block behind me, running to catch up. Mama sent him to try to bring me back, I bet. I won't go back. I can't. They've got to understand.

Liam catches up with me, out of breath. He hasn't played a game of stickball in over a year. "Want some company?" he says.

"Did Mama send you after me?"

"You the only one makes decisions around here? I got people to see today, too," he says, half-smiling.

"Okay then," I say, and start walking again.

"You headin' for the boulevard?" he says.

"Yeah."

"I'll take a ride with you."

"Okay," I say, and we make our way down 187th Street.

"Listen," he says, his voice low like someone plotting

something. "Have you still got that package I gave you?"

"What package?" I say.

"On the way to Daddy's, remember? We put it in your bag."

"Oh, I guess so." Our walk to Bryant Avenue two days ago comes back to me. It seems so long ago, but I remember the little brown package. I stop to lean against a parking meter so I can rummage through my bag. I find it at the bottom and take it out. Strands of my hair are wrapped around it, along with some cellophane from a candy wrapper.

I hand the package to Liam. He grabs it, and I see his face change, relax. He makes a little shush sound, like a sigh of relief. He hardly looks at it, just tucks it away quickly into his jacket pocket and starts walking again.

"I'm sorry," I say, catching up. "Did you need it? I forgot I had it."

"It's okay. It doesn't belong to me, that's all. I have to return it."

"Oh," I say, but I know he's lying. There's more to it than that. I can feel it, see it in his face.

"So how'd your friend get sick anyway?" he asks.

"She's not sick. She got hurt."

"Hurt how?"

"The guy thought her arm might be broken," I tell him.

"What guy?"

"The ambulance guy."

"What were you doin'? Climbin' trees or something?"

166

"She got beat up," I say. "I thought you knew." But I remember that he got in too late to hear Mama wailing about it all.

"Her old man?"

"No. It was these two kids. They came into her house, thought we had drugs there." Liam misses a step and gets quiet. "You know, like heroin or something." And even as I'm saying it, I see that he does know, and that he knows who those guys were. And I know now what's in that little package. "Liam . . ."

He stops, moves over to Musselli's hardware store and leans against the glass, like someone defeated. "Shit," he says. "I'm sorry."

"Are you crazy?" I whisper, but I feel as if I'm screaming at him. "Gettin' mixed up in stuff like that?"

"You gotta keep your mouth shut about this," he says, but he doesn't have to. He knows he doesn't. We never tell on each other. Ever.

"Is that why you came looking for me? Daddy said you went looking for me."

"That wasn't the only reason. Somebody had to find you. Runnin' off like that. Talk about crazy."

"It was crazy to go back to Daddy to begin with."

"It wasn't a big deal."

"You were bleeding." I try to keep my voice down, so no one will hear.

"I wasn't hurt. He cut my lip. No big deal, for Christ's sake." Liam gives me a hard look, wants me to drop it. He never likes to talk about what happens with Daddy. He gets mad when people do. I step away, look into Musselli's window. He must have two dozen hammers in there, each one a different size. Daddy has only one hammer, and he goes nuts when he can't find it. The whole house is mobilized to find it before he winds up losing it altogether and slamming somebody against a wall.

"I thought he was coming after me this time," I tell Liam.

He doesn't answer me at first. Then finally he says, "I guess I thought he was too." He jerks his head toward the direction we need to go. "Come on. Let's go."

We move on and stay quiet. The street is fairly empty, and there's the usual Saturday morning feeling about it, as if it's not quite awake yet. We walk past a tavern, with its small dark window lit by a Pabst Blue Ribbon sign, and I think of my father that night and wonder if Liam is too.

"Liam?" I say.

"Yeah."

"Why do you think he never hits me?"

"Luck of the draw. That's all."

"What do you mean?"

"You know. Random selection. He needs to have one thing in his life that can let him believe he's not a complete zero. And you're it."

"I'm it?"

"Sure. He doesn't do to you what he does to everyone else. That way he can pretend to himself he's not all bad after all."

I don't like Liam's answer. "How do you know that's the reason?"

"What's the matter?" he says. "You hopin' you were special or somethin'?"

"No," I say, but I did hope that. I always have. Though I never dare say it, never even dare believe it for sure. But sometimes, in the worst times, when I can't find anything good to believe about myself, I believe that. That I could be special to him somehow.

"Could have been any one of us," Liam says, and I swallow down whatever it is that's gathering in my throat like a pain. We don't say much for a block or so, until we reach Southern Boulevard and Liam stops to light a cigarette.

"Liam," I say.

"Yeah, what?"

"I'm sorry." I can see he doesn't understand what I mean. "I'm sorry I left you there like that."

His face changes, closes up. "Forget that," he says. "Forget him."

"I never should have done that."

"Everybody's got stuff they shouldn't have done. You'll have your share." He looks at me and I guess there's something in my face that makes him decide it's safe to accept my apology, to believe that I care about him, because he puts his arm around me. He's never done that before—ever—and I feel very special.

"You payin' my fare?" he says.

I roll my eyes. "If there's any money left after I go to the florist." A few doors ahead of us is Annie's Flower Shop. She's already got stuff outside, lots of mums in different colors.

Liam doesn't go into Annie's with me. He tells me to hurry and waits on the fender of a '57 Chevy. It only takes me a few minutes, because I know just what to ask for. Annie leads me to the back, to her flower fridge, and takes out a small bunch of the tiny purple flowers. She wraps them in paper with pink roses printed on it and asks me what the card should say. Her fingers are thin and dark, hardly thicker than her pen.

"Oh." I'm lost for a minute. "Just, 'Your friend Fiona,'" I tell her.

"'Your friend Fiona,'" she repeats as she writes it down. The pen moves very quickly.

"Yes. That's me."

"Well, you have a good day, Fiona."

Outside, the sun feels even warmer. Liam hops off the car. "Well, do we ride?"

"No," I tell him. "We walk."

"Sure, we walk," he says, and he sounds like an old philosopher who's learned to accept whatever comes his way.

We head down Southern Boulevard, under a sky that's wide and bright and warm. The rumble of the Number 3 bus gets louder behind us as it moves in close to find a place at the curb. The bus stops and opens its doors with a huge gassy sigh and lets an old man out the back door. He's short, with a bushy mustache and a huge nose and lots of gray hair that won't fit under his cap. He takes each step down slowly, painfully, each one a challenge. He barely makes it to the curb before the bus pulls away. That's where he stops, as if to rest, or maybe to try to remember where he's going, and looks at me.

I could be any kid walking with her big brother—a kid with a room, a dog, a phone number, things to do that day—but I'm not just any kid. I'm Fiona, the fair one, and I've got violets for Yolanda.